Go Ahead, Make My Bouquet

by

Misty Simon

Kissinger Kisses, Book Three

Go Ahead, Make My Bouquet

Cover Art by *Debbie Taylor*

The Wild Rose Press, Inc.
PO Box 708
Adams Basin, NY 14410-0708
Visit us at www.thewildrosepress.com

Publishing History
First Champagne Rose Edition, 2015
Print ISBN 978-1-5092-0126-6
Digital ISBN 978-1-5092-0127-3

Kissinger Kisses, Book Three
Published in the United States of America

Dedication

To Daniel for always being there

He ran a hand over his hair, not knowing where to start but knowing he had to say something to diffuse the tension thickening the air. "Look, I know I handled the other day badly."

She gave a little snort that could have been in disgust or a short burst of laughter. He had no idea which but had to power on, regardless.

"You do things to me, I admit it. If it were any other time, or a different set of circumstances, you know I would be on you faster than you could take your next breath."

There was a hitch in that next breath, a sign he was not doing this right, or he *was* doing it right, but not for the result he knew he should want—for her to go back to professional and friendly, instead of tempting him to break his own rules.

"I really need you to be here for Phoebe. I can't change how I feel about the best course of action with her. I have to give her my attention and my time. If you and I started anything, I wouldn't be doing that. I'd be jeopardizing the best thing that's come into her life recently."

"Sure." She crossed her arms over that chest he'd dreamed of. She had his own breath hitching, though more quietly.

"Look at how awkward we're being, and all we did is kiss. Can you imagine if we slept together and then you decided you didn't want us anymore? It's not just my own needs I have to think about."

"Why do you keep insisting that I'm going to be that fickle?"

Praise for Misty Simon

A MOTHER'S HEART: "[It] should be on everyone's 'To be read' list. It's also a great look into animal rescue."

~*Brenda Talley, The Romance Studio (5 Hearts)*
"If you enjoy romance stories about two people burned by relationships gone bad…then look no further."

~*Xeranthemum, Long and Short Reviews (4.5 Books)*
"A cute tale about a woman afraid to turn out like her mother and a man trying to take care of his children."

~*Debbie Gould, WRDF Review*
POISON IVY: "I loved this book. I was laughing during most of it."

~*Rae, My Book Addiction and More (4.5 rating)*
THE WRONG DRAWERS: "…a sass filled, one-two punch of delightfully quirky humor and intriguing mystery."

~*Jacki King, bestselling author*
WHAT'S LIFE WITHOUT THE SPRINKLES?: "Ms. Simon's writing has warmth, her characters seem like real people, and her plotting drew me in…."

~*Angie Just Read, The Romance Reviews*
~*~

Misty Simon's Other Books at The Wild Rose Press
A Mother's Heart
The Kissinger Kisses Series:
What's Life Without the Sprinkles?
Making Room at the Inn
The Ivy Morris Mysteries:
Poison Ivy
The Wrong Drawers
Something Old, Something Dead

Chapter One

"Not a single delivery for Casanova," Zoe Bradley grumbled to herself Saturday morning as she pulled a handful of orders off the shop's printer. "Again!" She knew she was being contrary. Up until two weeks ago, it irritated her every time she saw an order come in for the man she called Casanova, if only in her mind. But now that he hadn't sent a single order in, she was more irritated that he had probably gone somewhere else.

Decadence, the shop she shared with her sister and her best friend, was quiet at eight o'clock in the morning, so there was no chance of embarrassment in front of a client as she continued to talk to herself. "I was making three to five arrangements a week for months, and now nothing. He'd better not have found a new florist!"

She'd made almost forty bouquets for him in the four months since she'd had the unfortunate pleasure of meeting him and thinking he was a walking advertisement for a drool rag, only to find out that he was also a player. Thirty-seven bouquets to be exact…not that she was counting.

She walked back to the refrigerator and yanked bunches of flowers from their plastic buckets. Petals drifted to the floor, and she steadied herself. They weren't the offender, and it was a shame to take out her aggressions on the poor, helpless blooms.

Back at the front counter, she arranged the roses and lilies into a cut crystal vase. "Damn man might just get a talking to by yours truly if he's going somewhere else. Doesn't he have any loyalty to my best friend and her husband?" May was part owner of the shop, and her husband Brad had gone to college with Dexter Zegray, philanderer extraordinaire. That should mean that he only placed orders with Decadence, which happened to have a cake shop, a dress shop, and a flower shop all rolled into one convenient space.

"Who are you talking to?" May asked as she breezed in from across the hall. Petite and gently rounded with a belly full of baby, May had been a part-timer with Zoe and Claudia for five years, but had recently become part owner when Zoe's mom retired. She'd go back to part-time when the baby came, and Mona Bradley, Zoe's mom, would step in for six weeks.

"Ha! Myself."

May's oval face split into a wide grin. "You know that's the first step on your way to the men with the white jackets, honey."

"You're a riot. Dexter Zegray has not yet struck again. And he'd better soon, or I'm going after him for not being loyal to his friends." She held the orders out to May and waited until she took them to cross her arms over her chest. "Not a single order in two weeks, when I used to see them constantly. He'd better not be going to Betty Garvin down the street at Bloom Me This."

May leaned against the brass-and-glass refrigerated case Zoe used as a counter. "And you're complaining why? The guy irritated you constantly, and you bitched endlessly whenever an order came in. Shouldn't you be

2

rejoicing?"

"Okay, I'll give you that, but it's money out of our till that he has to be giving to someone else. How is that good?"

"Maybe he just doesn't need any more flowers. Brad said he had something going on, so maybe he finally got past the sending-flowers stage." May quirked an eyebrow, then waggled it. "And it's not as if you aren't a serial dater, too. You just don't think to send the men flowers after. Not even a thank-you card. That's a shame, honey. You need to find a man to not have to thank anymore."

Zoe sighed. "No, thanks."

"Are you sure you're not more put out that he might actually be involved with someone who doesn't need flowers?" May's cheeky smile tipped Zoe off that she was kidding, but Zoe still had to hold her tongue. She'd only wanted Dex for a brief second, until she'd found out who he was. Then he was instantly off limits. He'd made advances toward her, but she'd shut him down, knowing how he ran from one woman to the next without a hitch in his step.

"Maybe they'll have a falling out and you'll be making up 'Sorry' stuff in a few days, so then that'll be more money in your drawer. Plus, it's not like you want him." She smiled like the Cheshire cat. "Unless you do…"

Hell, no. She'd seen his kind before: charming, attentive—until they figured out what they wanted, realized it wasn't you, and then walked away. Zoe did not need that noise in her life anymore.

"I guess I could ask if Dexter has a girlfriend. Remember, he and Brad are friends." May's middle name had never been Subtle.

How could she forget when May brought it up all the time trying to get her to go out with him? May didn't believe he was a Casanova, just thoughtful. She'd even mentioned these could all be flowers for business acquaintances, and he was deliberately using Zoe's business to get her to notice him. But she knew better. And now he hadn't ordered in weeks.

She blocked the thought and went to the back again to pull more flowers, more carefully this time. It didn't matter why he wasn't ordering from her. And in fact it was less of a headache. A few times she had to talk herself down from sending along her own little note that said, "You're one of a bevy. Just FYI."

That, of course, would have been bad for business.

She marched back out to the front only to come face to face with the very devil himself.

And he had a baby carrier in his hand. What was this? Had all his philandering finally landed him in hot water?

"Are you sure you don't mind watching my niece, May? I know it's short notice, but I have a meeting this morning. I should be back no later than lunch. I can't thank you enough."

In the midst of trying not to notice him, Zoe checked her last mental remark. Niece, huh? She had no idea he even had any siblings. Then again, she'd never let him talk to her after that initial meeting, so that shouldn't come as too much of a surprise.

"Of course. It's not a problem at all." May smiled at him and then got a sly look in her eye. "We'll see you for dinner next Wednesday, though, right? We missed you this week."

He straightened his tie and avoided her stare. "I'll have to check my calendar. The last ten days have been hectic, but I promise to try."

"I suppose that's enough. I'll expect the story of where this niece I've never heard of came from, though."

May didn't know he had a niece either? Very interesting.

"That is a story for another day." He pulled the cuffs of his tailored shirt, and Zoe did her best not to notice the way the fabric fit across his chest. This was the man she had no intention of getting close to, darn it. The man who sent clutch after clutch of flowers to so many women she'd almost lost count. She did not need to notice his chest or the long fingers pulling the cuff links.

"I'll be back before you know it," he said with a smile that would melt the pants off a lesser, unmarried woman.

And then the baby in the carrier was passed over to May, who immediately started cooing nonsensical things. Dex hadn't even looked at Zoe yet. For all his blustering to May about wanting to get to know her, in the previous months, she wasn't even registering on his radar right now. She tried to tamp down the irritation, but it wasn't working very well.

He headed out the door without sparing her a glance, phone in hand and his thoughts obviously taken up by things other than her.

She couldn't decide if she was hurt or relieved that he seemed to have given up.

There wasn't much of a chance to wonder as May took the baby out of the carrier and cuddled her, turning her to face Zoe.

"Oh, Zoe, isn't she the cutest thing? There's no denying she's related to Dex, with those long dark lashes and the blue eyes, is there? Her name is Phoebe."

But May didn't seem to need an answer as she took the child around the shop, pointing out dresses, cupcake stands, and flowers as she passed through each part of Decadence, as if the tiny baby understood a word. She couldn't have been more than six months old. Where was the mom? The dad? Did Dex have a sister or a brother? Was he or she married? Did they live in the area? Maybe they had moved here recently, and Dex was in charge of babysitting but then had a meeting.

Although Zoe couldn't quite see putting Dex in charge of a child. Then again, what did she know about him to make that decision? She did know he was a player, but that didn't mean he wasn't a capable babysitter.

She was just about to go back to arranging flowers when May stumbled and almost dropped the baby. Zoe rushed around the counter and caught May's arm, removing the baby from her grasp as she nudged her into one of the visitor chairs Claudia had bought two months ago.

"What happened? Are you okay?" The baby grabbed the hair at Zoe's nape as Zoe leaned over to peer at May's pasty face.

"I...I'll be fine. I just need to sit for a minute." May began panting. It threw Zoe back to the Lamaze classes she'd taken with Claudia all those years ago when she'd been fifteen and Claudia's birthing room coach.

"That doesn't sound okay. Do you need me to call

Brad?"

"No. Hee hee hee. Ho ho ho."

"You sound like a deranged Santa Claus."

This time May laughed, easing up on her death grip on the arm of the chair. "Thanks so much for your encouragement."

Zoe straightened, untangling the little girl's fingers from her hair. Once that was done, she laid a hand on May's shoulder. "My pleasure, hon. Now, let me call Brad."

May shook her head. "No, I'm going to time these things for a little bit; then we'll go from there. I don't want to alarm everyone if it's just Braxton Hicks." But then her hands gripped her stomach, and she leaned forward, panting again.

"I'm calling Brad." Zoe dug her cell phone out of her back pocket. Everyone had Brad on speed dial at this point for just this kind of emergency.

"Please." May gripped her arm with a surprising strength. "Not yet."

"You're less than two minutes apart, May, even I know that's too close to ignore."

"But they just started. This could take hours. And Brad's working. I don't want to bother him if it's nothing."

"You're being ridiculous."

"Who's being ridiculous?" Claudia Bradley asked as she walked into the front of the shop from the storage space directly behind them. Her blonde hair was flawless and her smile was radiant. The darn thing had barely moved off her face since she and her best friend Nate had hooked up a couple of months ago. Not that Zoe blamed her. Nate was pretty yummy, and Claudia had finally realized it after eleven years. Zoe figured she'd be smiling, too, if she had that kind of man hanging around.

"May is being ridiculous," Zoe said, facing her sister, who registered shock as she took in the baby in Zoe's arms.

"Too much to explain right now. Later. Our immediate situation is that May is having contractions less than two minutes apart, yet she doesn't want me to call Brad. When she had these last week her OB said to go straight to the hospital once she hit less than three minutes between contractions."

Claudia crouched down next to May. "It's going to be okay, sweetie. Let's take you to the hospital just to be certain everything checks out. You know Brad will meet us there, and it'll all be good."

Tears shone in May's eyes, and her bottom lip quivered. "I don't know if I can do this."

"Of course you can, May. You are going to rock this thing." Claudia waved a hand behind her back, and Zoe stepped out of the room to place the call to Brad. They'd been best friends and sisters for their whole lives; no words were needed.

He answered on the first ring. "Is she okay?"

Zoe smiled. She loved Brad like a brother and was so happy he and May had found each other. "She is, but the contractions are coming fast and hard. Claudia's going to drive her to the hospital. Why don't you run home, grab the hospital bag, and meet them there?"

"Oh, okay. I should, I should do that. Yes, right now. I'll do that right now. Kiss her for me."

"Brad. Go!"

"Yep, going. Going right now. Have to go home

and get the bag, right?"

The smile on her face grew. "Yes, go home and get the bag. Meet them at the hospital."

"Will do. Bye." And he hung up, poor befuddled man.

The baby nested her fingers in the back of Zoe's hair, again, as they came back out into the front room.

"How far apart?" Zoe hunkered down next to May with the baby on her knee.

"Two minutes. We'd better go."

"Oh, God! Phoebe! I promised Dexter I'd watch her." May stood up to reach for the child.

"I've got her, May, no worries."

"But Dex…"

"Dex will be fine. I'm perfectly capable of caring for a kid until lunch, when he said he'd be back."

"But you don't mind?" She broke off to pant again, gripping her stomach.

"You'd better go before your water breaks. You don't want to be Claudia and have it break in some awkward place like at the movies watching some slasher rerun." Zoe rose from her crouch and hiked the baby up on her hip. She and Claudia shared a smile over the memory.

"But it wasn't supposed to happen like this!" May's wail set the baby—Phoebe—off into wailing too.

Zoe and Claudia exchanged a look, and Claudia stroked a hand over the soft, dark hair tickling Zoe's neck as Phoebe snuggled into her chest, weakly crying. "You're going to get in the car, May, and we're going to the hospital. It's all going to work out exactly as it should. Brad will be there, and we'll get to meet the little guy who's been kicking the stuffing out of your ribs. Zoe can handle Phoebe." Claudia shot Zoe a look that said she would have some explaining to do later. Zoe shrugged, because she didn't know much of anything, but she'd divulge whatever she did know when the current crisis was taken care of.

Zoe came over and planted a kiss on May's cheek. "Brad said to kiss you for him, but I'm not going to do it like he will when you get to the hospital, which you should leave for right now."

And they did, leaving Zoe waving out the front window as Claudia ushered a panting May to her car. Leaving her with a baby girl she knew nothing about, who belonged to a man she didn't know much about, either.

First things first. She decided to call and leave him a message that there had been a change of plans, so he wasn't angry when he came back to find May gone and Zoe with Phoebe. They'd had enough heated exchanges that she thought it might be a good idea to warn him.

Her call went straight to voicemail, which was fine with her. Now what to do with a six-month-old little girl for the next few hours while she waited for news on May and for Dex to come back?

She turned to where she'd placed Phoebe in the carrier and found her fast asleep. Well, that answered that question. She'd quietly finish the rest of the orders and then gear herself up to ask Dex who he was using to send his bevy of beauties flowers these days.

Chapter Two

Dexter Zegray drove through yet one more section of town, hoping against hope to spot his brother's car. He'd been searching for ten days. Ten long days in which he'd also called and texted and bugged any person who even knew Ethan's name, and all to no avail. Who knew a nineteen-year-old could be so good at disappearing from the face of the earth?

Slowing his Land Rover, Dex took a right onto Orchard Street and finally admitted defeat. After his meeting this morning, he'd taken the time to run around town one more time. He'd been all over the town of Kissinger, in and out of alleys, peeking in garages and carports, looking for the Rambler he'd helped Ethan fix up for his sixteenth birthday, but had come up empty. Again.

He rested his head on the steering wheel and just took a moment. On Tuesday last, he and Ethan had been celebrating the job offer Ethan had secured as a paid apprentice at a small machine shop. Dex had been so proud of how far his brother had come in the year since they'd moved to this small Pennsylvania town and away from Washington, D.C. The last seven years had not been easy, with their parents dying and leaving a twelve-year-old Ethan in the care of Dex, who had been in his last years of law school. They'd muddled through until Ethan's junior year in high school, when Dex saw patterns and heard excuses he didn't like and couldn't stomach. At the end of that school year, Dex had moved Ethan away from the influences that were bad for him and into this small community, where he had thrived. He'd thought they left D.C. behind.

And they had. Until Ethan's ex-girlfriend showed up on their doorstep, baby in tow, and handed her over, rights and all, without looking back.

They'd both been shocked. Dex rhythmically tapped his fist on the dashboard. They'd both stood and stared at each other as Delly Ferndale got back into her rattletrap car and took off, leaving the six-month-old Phoebe behind with some diapers, some formula, a trash bag of clothes, and one blanket that had seen better days. Oh, and a handwritten note on a sheet of notebook paper, relinquishing all rights to the small baby.

But they'd rallied together as the clock ticked toward midnight on a weekday when Dex would have to be up and ready to face clients the next day. They'd plotted and planned and worked out a schedule and a strategy that would make this work.

Or at least that was what Dex had been thinking when he went to bed, only to be awakened by a screaming child at three a.m., a child with a note pinned to her telling him Ethan needed time to think and would be back when he was ready.

Dex punched the steering wheel this time. "Dammit!" he yelled in the car with the windows rolled up. "Dammit," he said more quietly as he straightened his tie and took the car out of park.

He'd taken a week's vacation on a moment's notice, so thankful his boss, Al Greenburg, had been willing to let his relatively new partner shift all his work to the older man with less than a handful of sentences. Dex had spent all that time with Phoebe in the car, scouring any and every section of town, even taking one day to go back to Ethan's old haunts in D.C. But nothing turned up. And the damned kid would not answer his phone.

There was nothing more to do. He'd have to talk with Sam, the man who had offered Ethan a job, and that was all there was to it. His stomach knotted at the prospect, but he couldn't keep his friend in the dark any longer. He doubted anything could be salvaged after this, but that was the price of leaving town without a word. Eighteen months of good had come to an end.

Pulling into Sam's driveway, Dexter released a long breath and shot his cuffs. Hopefully Sam would understand. If he didn't, there wasn't much that could be done. There was still hope Ethan would return, but it was getting slimmer every day.

"Hey, buddy!" Sam Locke strode from the huge barn he called a shop with his hand extended and a smile on his face. "It's good to see you. Is Ethan looking forward to getting started next month? I have orders pouring in that will show him the ropes faster than a reluctant seaman."

Dex tried for a smile that matched that of the big man opposite him, but he couldn't pull it off. "Can we talk?"

"Of course." Sam's face turned serious, and he walked past Dex, then on into the big clapboard house where he lived.

Dex followed along, mentally preparing his case for waiting for Ethan to return, yet knowing there was no real convincing evidence that it was ever going to happen.

"What's up, my friend?" Sam asked as he dug into the refrigerator. "Soda? You look like you could use a beer, but it's only about ten in the morning."

"No, thanks, to either." A beer wouldn't solve anything, no matter the time of day. *And I have a baby to take care of now.* His whole life had changed, and he wouldn't be getting it back any time soon, no matter if Ethan came home or not.

"So lay it on me. Whatever it is, it's got to be weighty if you came out here instead of giving me a buzz." Sam took a sip from his own can of soda, then held it against his chest.

No time like the present. "Ethan has left. I don't know when he'll be back. I hope he'll return before he's supposed to start working with you, but I can't guarantee it. I'm sorry."

"I take it this isn't a planned senior trip then, huh?"

Dex pinched the bridge of his nose and bowed his head. "No. He took off ten days ago, and I haven't heard from him since. I didn't want to leave you hanging, in case he doesn't come back. I wish I had different news." Boy, did he ever. He was going to wring Ethan's neck when he came home.

"Can I ask what sent him out? Was he afraid to apprentice? Afraid to become an adult, so he ran?"

"I wish it was that damn simple." Dex blew out a breath and leaned against the opposite counter. "Apparently before we left D.C. he must have gotten his then-girlfriend pregnant. She said nothing to him about it. We weren't aware of the fact until she came to our door to drop the baby off, stating she was done taking care of 'his brat' and he could have her now. She signed over all rights and left without even looking at the little girl."

"Huh." Sam took another swallow of soda. "Just left her? You're sure it's his?"

He and Ethan had been over this, but, since Phoebe was the spitting image of Ethan when he was a baby, there was no denying the genes had been passed along. "Yes, there's no doubt. But he must have taken off in the middle of the night, because the child woke up screaming. I called for him, but he never answered. I picked her up, called his cell, and it just rang endlessly. I was bewildered until I found the note in her playpen. He needs time to figure out what he's going to do."

"And while he'd doing that, you're left holding the bag—or the baby, as the case may be."

Dex crooked up one side of his mouth in an approximation of a smile. "I guess so. She's been good, but in ten days I've made no headway on finding him, or a nanny to care for her, and now I have to disappoint you also." He took a breath to calm his rising anger. "And all because he doesn't know what to do." It didn't work. "Which is bullshit. It's obvious what he needs to do. He just needs to be man enough to come back and do it."

Sam eyed him. "You know that, and I know that, but he might need a little time." Sam tipped his can toward Dex. "He's nineteen. What were you doing at nineteen?"

Dex blew out an irate breath. "I wasn't abandoning a baby to someone else's care."

"But you were at college, right? Living it up? Not having a care in the world except what your next grade was."

That was true except that he'd also been running from his alcoholic parents and a home that he hadn't been able to wait to leave. He'd even moved into an apartment right off campus and worked full time over the summer under the pretense that he was trying to settle into the new town before he got started studying. It hadn't been a lie precisely, but it was escape, nonetheless. And he'd had no intention of ever going back, until the fateful day when he'd received the call his parents were dead and Ethan needed him. Twelve to his twenty-four, Ethan had only been six when Dex left for college, and they'd known almost nothing about each other, since Dex had not come home for breaks or holidays. Then he'd been faced with an angry, unknown preteen. But he'd stepped up to the plate, dammit!

"I might have been carefree at nineteen, but when he needed me I took the semester off and came back for him. Hell, I changed schools so he could stay in his house."

"Not your house, too?"

"No." He folded his arms over his chest. He was not going there. This was not about him but about his brother, who needed to get his ass home and take some responsibility.

"Got it," Sam said, then took another swallow from the can. "Look, I can keep the job open for a few weeks for him. I can't make a promise for longer than that. I let everyone know I was open to more orders as soon as I signed your brother on, and I can't let them down, or turn work away. You understand?"

"Absolutely." Dex stuck his hands into his pockets. "I'm hoping he'll be back before then, but I can't make any promises either. Please don't worry if you find someone qualified to help."

He left shortly after that and jerked his car door shut. Sam had a business to run. He couldn't be expected to hold up this growth he'd been planning for, just because Ethan wasn't man enough to come home.

Dex had seen a phenomenal opportunity when the gruff guy had come into the law office to ask about incorporation and laws for having employees. Ethan had always had a fascination with building things, and there wasn't a better person to take his brother under his professional wing. Ethan was messing up everything by being a coward.

But was he being fair? Dex tried to shrug off the thought as he drove downtown, but it stuck like a burr. He had been free of responsibility at nineteen, and Ethan had been as shocked as he was to see the baby dropped on their doorstep. If he'd been called to help with Ethan at nineteen, would he have fought so hard for him? Gone to such lengths to keep him when it could have been easier to let him go into the system and given to a family who would care for him?

It was a non-question. Dex had done enough research into law at that point and enough job shadowing to realize that the system wasn't kind to many of the inhabitants. People tried, and some of them did a wonderful job, but more used it as a means to make money and never really cared. He'd hopped into his car with the phone still on his ear, when the call had come in about his parents' deaths, and hit the gas to get to his brother. No other path had occurred to him despite the distance and the fact he hadn't seen the boy in six years at that point.

He just hoped his example would eventually come across to Ethan and remind him that sometimes you had to make sacrifices for those who were smaller than you.

His phone beeped with a message. He'd put it on vibrate when he'd been in talking with Sam, not wanting to interrupt their conversation, and sure that Ethan would not call at the very moment Dex didn't have it on. But someone had called. He put it on speaker in his car and was surprised to hear Zoe Bradley's voice come through his sound system.

"Hey, Dexter, um, just wanted to let you know I have Phoebe. May went into labor. Claudia took her to the hospital, and Brad's meeting them there. I didn't know exactly when you were coming back, but I didn't want you to be, um, irritated when you showed and saw that May had left the baby with me. We're having a great time, and I'm rattling along. Anyhoo, see you later. Bye."

That voice had done things to his equilibrium for months. She was the oddest combination of plucky and prickly, and he'd thought many times about what a challenge it would be to unwrap the layers that made up Zoe Bradley. Sadly, with this new addition he would have no more time for pursuit. It hadn't worked for him in the months since he'd met her anyway, so perhaps this was a blessing in disguise. Regardless, he decided to go take the child off Zoe's hands. She couldn't be happy to have been forced to take over the burden he'd laid on May, and he was sure she would rather be with her friend at the impending birth of her child.

Speaking into the empty car, he asked his phone to call her back.

"Decadence, Zoe here."

"Dex here."

She muffled what he was sure would have been a snicker. Not completely immune to some silliness then. Not that the observation would help him at this point.

"Hey, Dex. Did you get my message?"

He mentally shook his head. No flirting. There was not a worse scenario to try to further his pursuit of her when he figured he was going to be celibate for a good long while. "I did get your message, and I appreciate it. I should be there in about thirty minutes. I'll cut things short after making one last stop so you don't have to watch Phoebe and can go be with May."

"There's no rush. Phoebe is adorable company, and Claudia just called with an update that things are going slow. It could be hours. I wouldn't know what to do with myself if I just sat there making funny breathing noises with May."

He figured she intended for him to laugh, so he did, just a chuckle. "If you're sure it's not an inconvenience, then I have a few other things to do."

And here was one more person he was depending on to take up slack that shouldn't have been his in the first place. He gripped the steering wheel so hard his knuckles turned white.

"No big." He could hear the smile in her voice.

A smile that he'd wanted aimed at him for the last five months, but for some reason she never gave it to him. He had a feeling she wouldn't be smiling if she knew the whole of the story about how he got this niece.

"I shouldn't be too long, if you really don't mind."

"It's okay, Dex, I really don't mind. Now, let me get back to her, and we'll see you whenever you're ready. I'll call if I hear anything more about May."

She disconnected the call, and he sat for another moment on the side of the road. He would do what was necessary, because he always had, but somehow he was going to have to let go of this anger. The child didn't deserve it, and it would serve no purpose.

With a deep breath, he put the car back in drive and moved forward. It was all going to have to be forward from here. He had a nanny to hire, a brother to find, a house to run, and a job to keep if he had time when he was done with everything—and everyone—else who needed a piece of him.

Chapter Three

Phoebe played contentedly with her toes in her car seat as Zoe began a flower arrangement for the Newton's charity gala for juvenile diabetes. She had forty-two more to go. Her hands were cramping, but it was for a good cause, and a good chunk of cash.

Decadence was doing well for itself. May was having a baby, Claudia was getting married in two months and had moved into Nate's big house with Justin, and Zoe was living by herself for the first time ever. It should have been good... No, it was good.

But she welcomed the distraction from her thoughts and her cramping hands when Phoebe began to cry.

"What's up, sweet baby?" She unstrapped the little girl from her carrier, cooing as she snuggled her against her chest. Bouncing her a little, she searched in the reusable grocery bag Dex had left with the carrier and came up with a bottle and a hand towel that looked like it might have come from a kitchen drawer.

Popping the bottle into the microwave, she gave it a few seconds at a time, not sure how long it needed to warm but knowing she didn't want to scorch it.

Five seconds at a time seemed to take forever as the child continued to cry. She remembered those days with Justin screaming at the top of his pretty impressive lungs as he waited very impatiently to be fed. They'd still been living with their parents because Claudia was going to classes to refine her cake-making technique, and Zoe was still in high school. But she'd spent many nights rocking Justin in his bouncy seat with one hand while she used the other to write out history notecards and color code maps of Eastern Europe. She'd also been called on to give him bottles when Claudia was at class in the evenings and couldn't be there to breastfeed him.

The crying was the same, too, though Phoebe's lungs weren't nearly as strong as Justin's had been. Poor little thing was mewling like a kitten.

Finally the bottle was ready. Zoe tested it on her wrist and found it to be warm but not hot. She popped it into the little girl's mouth and enjoyed the blessed silence that blanketed the room, leaving only the soft background music. They'd found a station that did popular songs with only strings. It was beautiful, and now she could hear it again.

Phoebe slurped and slurped at the bottle, finally settling into a rhythm and quieting. Her blue eyes drifted closed with her fist curled at her chin.

So cute. Zoe ran a finger through the dark brown hair curling over her head. What was the story here? It felt like more was going on, especially because Dex had missed dinner with May and she had never heard of this baby before. Hmm. Not that it was any of her business, of course, but it was still curious.

Phoebe's mouth fell open with only an ounce left in the bottle. Zoe hadn't had a chance to burp her, but she didn't want to wake her up just yet. She'd be okay for the moment. Placing her back in her carrier, Zoe found a blanket in the grocery bag and placed that on top of her. She dug around in the bag some more, but found no stuffed animal, or cuddly anything, beyond the blanket. There were a handful of diapers, though, two changes of clothes, and another bottle in the cooler at the bottom of the bag. If nothing else, Dex knew how to pack the essentials.

Speak of the devil. Dex emerged from a car she would have easily placed him in if asked. The Land Rover was big, hulking, and suited Dexter Zegray, Attorney at Law, to a T.

And there he was, rounding the hood of the car, his step slowing as he came to the sidewalk, where he straightened his tie and then pinched the bridge of his nose before standing straight and walking the last few steps to the front door of Decadence.

There was definitely something more going on here. And she shouldn't wonder so much what it was...

He entered the shop with purpose. "Zoe, first, thanks,"

"Shh," she said quickly, pointing to the sleeping Phoebe. "Why don't we walk over to the cake side and leave her for a moment."

"Will she be okay by herself?" He peered over the side of the carrier set on the counter, but kept his hands clasped behind his back.

"Yes," she said simply before she led the way to Claudia's side of the store and took a seat at one of the chairs at the café tables designed for cake taste-testing.

"Thank you for watching her."

"You already said that." She wanted to smile at him, but looking at him reminded her that she found him incredibly attractive and incredibly irritating. A cute niece did not negate the fact that this man was a philanderer.

"Thank you, again, anyway."

"Not a problem at all." She sat back in her chair to eye him. Somehow she had forgotten who he was as she'd cared for Phoebe. But one charming little girl, and a situation that she hadn't yet grasped the particulars of, did not make up for all the bouquets she'd made for a whole lot of women. Nor did it make up for the fact that he was no longer using her services for those bouquets. Part of her wanted to bring it up, but the other part wasn't sure she wanted the answer. Perhaps he had finally settled on one woman who didn't need flowers every day to be wooed, like May had suggested. She didn't want to know that, either.

"Your niece was an angel today," she said to cover what was rapidly becoming an awkward silence.

"Thank you. She does seem to be very content for being only six months old, and with her circumstances."

The opening she'd been looking for! "What circumstances?"

He made a point of glancing down at the watch on his strong wrist. "Look, I didn't realize what time it is. I have to go."

"Oldest trick in the book, Zegray, and you're not going to get away with it." She fixed him with a determined stare. "What circumstances?"

"Not that it's any of your business, but I'll be caring for Phoebe for a few weeks until her father comes home."

"And where's her father? I didn't even know you had a brother."

"I'm surprised you remember my last name, for the few times you've actually deemed it okay to speak with me," he muttered.

"Of course I remember your last name, it's on the credit card every time I run it, isn't it? Not that I have been doing that lately since you seem to have gone to another florist."

He blew out a breath, ruffling the dark hair that had flopped onto his brow. He changed the subject. "Again, not that it's any of your business, but I am hoping to have an initial phone interview with a potential nanny today. I don't want to be late. This is the third. I hope it's the charm."

Why was he hiring a nanny for his brother's child? Why did he have his brother's child at all? Unless the brother was in the military. But then where was the girl's mother? She let the topic slide for now, thinking she could get info out of May at a later date. And pressing would feel too much like she cared about him and his situation—which, of course, she didn't.

"Well, good luck with that. Claudia never used a nanny, so I have no idea how that works."

"How did she work and go to school?"

"She had me." A twinkle lit those navy blue eyes, and it was all she could do not to squirm in her chair.

"Can I have you, too?"

Crossing her arms and frowning at him did not accomplish what she thought it would.

His eyes lit with the same mischief they had on the first day she'd met him in her uncle's office and realized he was the man she called Casanova. "Come on, you could be my nanny. Live-in or not, your choice. I'm sure you're great with kids, and I wouldn't mind coming home to that face every night, especially if I could get you to smile at me like you were at Phoebe before I came in."

"Please. Put it away." She said it quickly to head off anything more he might have said.

"Put what away?"

"The fake charm. I'm not going to be your nanny. Hopefully the phone call will go well and everything will be settled."

"I wasn't being charming. You wouldn't be able to resist me if I were being charming."

She had little doubt about that. "Anyway, she's been fed and is ready to go."

"When you said Claudia had you, what did you mean?"

She barely resisted rolling her eyes. At this point she just wanted him out of the shop. His dark hair was a little mussed, his tie not exactly straight, and all she wanted to do was sit in his lap and straighten it as she pulled him in for a kiss. That thought could just go the way of the ends of the flower stalks—straight into the trash. She did not want him, would never again want him.

"I mean that Justin used to run around here, and we all watched him. Claudia was working, I was going to school, but we traded off with my mother, and it worked out for us."

"And you don't think it could work out now? You could be my babysitter, if you don't like the word nanny." He smiled at her then, but it wasn't the real thing, more like what he thought might win her over.

"Dex, I can't be your anything. Now," she said as she rose from her chair, went back to her portion of the store and grabbed the grocery bag. "You had better get going. Maybe you can get Phoebe to stay asleep for the call. She went down about thirty minutes ago, and most kids take at least an hour-long nap. I'd take advantage of that, if I were you, and not dally." She was all business, packing the few things he'd brought back into the bag and looping it over his strong arm. She did not—would not—think about the strength of the bicep she had just brushed up against, or even that probably hours after he had showered he still smelled of sandalwood with a hint of mystery underneath.

"Here's your hat, what's your hurry?" he asked.

"No, I did what you asked May to do, and now I have to get back to work. Your hurry is that you have a phone call with someone who I know will be perfect for you and Phoebe until her father comes home." She used just her fingertips to cocoon the baby in her blanket and leaned forward to whisper a kiss over her sweet-smelling forehead. If ever she had wanted to take on another child, this was the one, with her silly, gummy smile and her fascination with her toes.

She looked up in time to see a brief flash of pain and uncertainty cross Dex's face. Then it was gone as he nodded to her.

"Can I at least take a minute to order May flowers?"

"I thought you were going to another florist."

"Never," he said. "You have my credit card on file, I'm sure. Make it beautiful, as you always do."

And then he walked out the door with Phoebe in her carrier, snoozing away.

Zoe did not have the time, or the inclination, to find out what the look had meant, or why it pained her to see it on his handsome face. He was not her business, and neither were his troubles. She would simply tell herself that until she believed it.

****

Phoebe stayed asleep as Zoe had predicted. She'd slept the whole way home and during his conversation with a certain Mrs. Pike. The woman was in her fifties and should have been perfect, with her credentials and her previous experience, but Dex did not end up inviting her for a real interview at his home. Her voice was too harsh, too gravelly, and some of her answers had been too uptight for his liking. He knew what he wanted.

A swift vision of Zoe rose in his mind, leaning over Phoebe and tucking the blanket in around her as she bent to place a kiss on the little girl's head and said goodbye. He shut it down. He'd wanted Zoe long before now, and she had rebuffed him over and over again, all without ever telling him why. He'd thought it was a game of cat-and-mouse and had been willing to play along to see exactly how long it would take him to catch the intriguing woman, but that time was past now. He had a child to raise if he couldn't find his brother. And maybe even if he could.

He laid his head down on his desk, blowing out a breath and hoping to dispel some of the tension with the air. Of course, it didn't work that way.

His shoulders were tight, his neck a mass of solid rock, and his forehead pounding with a headache that wasn't going to go away any time soon.

Checking on Zoe, he found her still asleep in her carrier. He'd thought about removing her to the playpen Delly had dumped in the family room. They had no crib yet; Dex had kept hoping Ethan would come home so they could go shopping for his daughter together. But

Dex couldn't put it off much longer. He'd already bought a second round of diapers, with the help of a bubble-gum-chewing girl at the local grocery store. He'd had no idea what size to buy or that there were so many sizes to consider. A woman coming down the aisle with her own baby had saved both him and the clerk by pulling out the right size and smiling at him. She'd asked if it was his first time shopping for the wife, and he had not corrected her, just smiled and thanked her. The less anyone knew about this, the better off he was. He had not had to deal with censure, or people looking down at him, for the last year. No one here knew his parents had been functioning drunks with little to no regard for keeping house or a checkbook. That lack of knowledge had been one of the major draws to this town.

Forcing those thoughts aside before he got too far down that lane, he grabbed a soda from the refrigerator and came back to sit in his leather office chair and stare at the baby in her carrier.

The soft way Zoe had kissed her forehead echoed in his mind and forced him to think about the fact that he hadn't kissed the baby at all. He hadn't even held her if he didn't have to. Yes, he'd fed her a bottle and changed her, but he also let her sit in her car carrier or lie in the playpen far more than he should. He always had some excuse, but that's exactly what they were, excuses.

On impulse, he tried Ethan's cell, not really thinking that this time out of the hundreds of times he'd dialed before would be the time Ethan would pick up.

And so he wasn't prepared when a gruff voice answered, "I told you I needed time, Dex."

Dex fumbled the phone and almost hung up by accident. He never did anything by accident.

"Shit." He picked the phone up from the floor where it had dropped. "Ethan? Ethan, are you there?"

"I answered the phone, didn't I?"

"Yes, it's just that you haven't in ten days. I'd begun to wonder if something had happened to you."

Ethan's laugh was harsh and derisive. "I think enough has already happened. Don't you?"

Pinching the bridge of his nose was not going to work this time. He drew in a breath and let it out. "Ethan, I believe things have happened. I understand that this was a shock to you, and that it was unexpected." Though he tried to keep his voice calm, as he would in a courtroom when he was trying to make a logical point, he couldn't seem to do it this time. "But you left in the middle of the night without a word except a ridiculous note saying you needed time to think." With each word he got louder and louder, until finally he hit a crescendo and the shit hit the fan at the same time. "What the hell does that mean?" Phoebe started screaming, Ethan was swearing and Dex was ready to throw his phone against the wall. "Get the hell back here!"

But he was speaking to a dead line.

Gently placing the phone on his cherrywood desk, he massaged his forehead and went for Phoebe. No use both of them being miserable.

****

Lucinda Reilly Blanchard came into the world at 5:30 in the evening, squalling like a champion. Zoe heard her from her perch on a plastic chair outside the room. She and Claudia looked at each other and shared a huge smile. Zoe had arrived only ten minutes before, after closing down the shop.

Claudia had come out when Zoe peeked her head into the room to find May struggling mightily and swearing just as mightily at a smiling Brad.

"Shopping and dinner," Claudia said, grabbing her purse. "It'll probably be a little while before they have all their measurements and get May cleaned up. And you and I have some talking to do."

When Zoe stuck her tongue out, Claudia rolled her eyes and grabbed her arm. "Childish gestures are not going to get you out of spilling the whole story about this morning. I want to hear how you managed the delicious Dexter Zegray."

A determined Claudia was a forbidding opponent, especially since she had hooked up with Nate and was on the way to her very own happily ever after. All of a sudden she wanted Zoe to be in a relationship, too.

She would give Claudia the minimum and fend her off as best she could. Dex was not for her, never would be. Zoe had actually been dating someone up until about two months ago, a man she had thought perhaps would be the one, but yet again they'd parted ways, friends, and he'd just asked her to make a beautiful arrangement for his future mother-in-law. Soon enough she would probably be providing all the flowers for the wedding of another ex-boyfriend marrying the girl he dated right after her. It was the twelfth such happening in the last four years.

If she didn't know better, she'd think she was some sort of tester wife. See if you like this kind of girl? No? Then go for the exact opposite and your prize is true love, dear gentleman!

The pattern was clear, and no one had said anything to her, but the truth was inescapable. She was the Pickle Jar Loosener, and she wouldn't do that for Dexter Zegray.

Chapter Four

"So how did it go today?"

Claudia sat across from Zoe with some sort of wrap thing the cafeteria worker swore by. Said it was the best thing they made. Zoe had opted for a grilled cheese. Only once in her life had she had a bad grilled cheese at a restaurant. It tended to be the one thing no one could screw up.

Claudia munched and chewed as Zoe picked apart her sandwich. Was Phoebe happy right now? Thinking about May and Lucinda had made her wonder how the little girl was faring with Dex. It wouldn't help to think about it.

Zoe popped a piece of grilled cheese into her mouth, knowing that whatever words came out they could be construed the wrong way. Ever since Claudia and Nate had hooked up and made the perfect little family that should have been years ago, she had been on Zoe's tail to find herself a special guy. It wasn't that she hadn't looked, Zoe thought as she chewed, peering at Claudia. She had looked, and often; it just had never been her who was special enough to keep the attention of the guys she dated. She could snag them but never completely reel them in. That was for the girl after her to do.

Claudia stared back. This wasn't going to be easy, then.

"I watched the little girl, and then Dexter came to pick her up. Nothing more than that."

"Nothing?"

"Well, he did ask if he could keep me, and if I'd be interested in being his live-in nanny, but honestly I think something more is going on here. I could swear he was just trying to deflect me."

"He wanted to keep you?" Claudia snickered. Of course that was the one thing she picked up on.

"Yeah, that's what he said, but only after I asked what happened to Phoebe's parents."

Claudia cocked her head to the side and took another bite of her wrap. "Why do you think he's avoiding the subject? Do you know if his brother is younger or older?"

"No, I was going to ask, but then May went into labor, and the question was lost."

A particularly gooey piece of grilled cheese came off the plate, and she stuffed it into her mouth. She had always been a curious one, and the way Dex had deflected her question made her more than curious—it made her downright rabid to know what the story was.

"Did he say what he's been doing with the baby, or what he'll do going forward?"

Trust Claudia to hit that one spot Zoe wasn't sure about. It's what sisters did.

"He was interviewing a nanny today by phone. Hopefully she'll work out. I guess his vacation is all used up, and he can't exactly have a baby in the law office with him while he's conducting business. He even asked if you had had Justin in the shop when he was little, and if maybe I could watch her during the day." She stopped mid-laugh when Claudia gripped her arm.

"You should do it. You should watch her for Dex. You know how to take care of kids, and we can all take turns if you get super busy. It would be like old times." She got this misty-eyed look to her that Zoe did not trust. Was it because she was dreaming of wedding music and flowers for Zoe and Dexter, or because she missed having a small baby in the shop?

It didn't matter. She wasn't doing it. "No, I have too much going on, and I'm sure Dexter Zegray is the kind of person who would need impeccable credentials and probably some sort of master's degree before he'd actually let me watch the child. Hell, he didn't even ask me today, he asked May, and then unforeseen circumstances made it necessary for me to take over."

"Don't undervalue yourself, Zoe."

"I'm not," Zoe said, following the words with a forced laugh. "I'm just being honest. Anyway, it doesn't matter. I'm sure he'll have found someone else by now, and hopefully it will work out for them."

Grilled cheese and wrap consumed, they made a quick stop at the gift shop, where Zoe wanted to buy one of everything. She settled on a monkey with a flower on its belly for Lucinda, deliberately leaving on the shelf the turtle she thought Phoebe would love. She probably wouldn't see the little girl again. Why buy her a toy?

As soon as they entered the hospital room, they gathered to May's side, who then told Brad to go get some coffee and take a break.

He looked ready to argue as Claudia and Zoe cooed over Lucinda. She looked just like a little gnome and was bald as a cue ball.

Brad must have thought better of arguing. He gave a mock salute to the three of them and kissed the baby on the head before leaving. "I'll be back in fifteen minutes. I'm not leaving my girls for longer than that tonight."

May sighed as he left and blew him a kiss. But as soon as the door shut, she was all business, snuggling Lucinda into her arms and giving Zoe the beady-eyed stare.

"Now, I'll have to be quick because Brad didn't tell me I couldn't tell you, but he also didn't tell me I could. This is emergency-girl-meeting time."

Zoe could do without an emergency girl meeting that was going to revolve around her. Wasn't it enough that she wanted to just make flower arrangements, try to get used to living by herself for the first time in her entire life, and enjoy her friends? Why did it always have to be about a guy?

"This isn't about the man," May said as if reading her mind. "It's about the baby. Hear me out before you say anything, though."

Zoe opened her mouth and got shot down before she could even get her tongue moving.

"I said hear me out. I'm the new mother and queen for the day. It's the least you can do." The smile might have softened the words if Zoe hadn't felt like she was in the spotlight of her friend's and sister's meddling. It was fine for her to meddle but not to be meddled with.

"Now, Brad told me that this baby was a surprise of thunderous proportions. Apparently Dex's nineteen-year-old brother is the reason they moved here in the first place. Dex had to get him out from under the influence of some kids who were leading him down the wrong path." She snuggled Lucinda in closer and implored Zoe with her eyes.

"He left behind an ex, too. Ethan was ready to go when she broke it off, and he came willingly because he knew that where he was heading in D.C. was not where he wanted to be."

Zoe settled into a chair. They only had about ten minutes left, but May could get longwinded when she had something to say.

"He's been doing well. He graduated in the top twenty-five percent of his class and went to Vo-Tech to learn machining. Dex had him all set up for an internship with his friend at a machine shop." She bit her lip. "And then the ex dropped off Phoebe, a child neither of them knew about. She never told Ethan she was pregnant when she left. But when she pulled up to the house, she apparently told them both that she was done being tied down with the brat and was not going to suffer raising her. Ethan could do it."

Zoe couldn't help the gasp. Who did that? What kind of cruel, heartless woman would just turn her back on a child because it was inconvenient? Claudia had been in the same position, though in different circumstances, but it amounted to the same thing. And she and Zoe would die before they would have let someone take Justin away from them.

"So she drops the baby off, and Ethan and Dex are at a loss what to do. They talk, as Dex usually is a big talker, about the future and how they are going to handle things. Phoebe's screaming in the middle of the night, and Dex waits for Ethan to get her. When he doesn't, Dex goes himself. Only to find a note pinned to the old playpen saying Ethan needs time to think, and if the ex doesn't have to take care of her then it's not fair that Ethan has to, either."

Another gasp, this one from Claudia. Zoe was too shocked to even move her mouth, much less her throat.

"And so now Dex has had Phoebe for ten days, using his vacation to look for Ethan and try to find someone to come in and help him. But no one is the right person for the baby, and he has run out of time. Brad said he had to go tell the machinist about the change in plans today, and he was pissed. After everything he's done for that boy, and he walked."

And that was what he had been trying to hide from her. That was why Dex had turned all flirty with her and wanted to take her home. He was perfect in many ways, seemed to live a charmed life, and yet this was a side she'd had no idea was within him and his home.

Did it change anything, though? Yeah, she felt sorry for him, but she was not going to watch a baby all day long while he worked just because no one seemed right for him. He might just need to unbend a bit to find someone who was okay.

But that thought seized her stomach. After all the abandonment, Phoebe deserved someone who would care for her. Could Zoe be that person? It put a lump in her throat.

She didn't want to be involved with Dex, but she knew herself well enough, and had been through plenty, to know she was capable of keeping herself separate and only letting in those who mattered. She could let Phoebe in without Dex, couldn't she?

Claudia and May were staring at her, and it made her want to squirm.

"Will you do it?" her sister asked, her heart on her

sleeve.

"Will you?" May asked, cuddling her newborn to her chest.

Would she? she asked herself—and then wanted to stomp around the room that was thick with guilt. She hated guilt. Hated getting guilted into things. She was a grown woman who could make her own decisions. *But Phoebe isn't*, her mind whispered. Damn mind!

"I'll think about it," she said finally. She held up her hand like a traffic cop. "Don't push me. Just let me think about it." And she walked out the door, not certain what exactly she should do and wondering why simply watching a baby was causing this much commotion.

Strolling down the quiet corridor of the maternity ward, she stopped to look at the new crop of babies who had been born today. So innocent, hopefully so loved. Would Phoebe have that? Dex had barely touched her, hardly even looked at her when they'd been in Decadence earlier. Was that the same as at home? Did he just need a little time? Or did he look at her as a burden, as everyone else apparently did?

There were many things that could go wrong with watching the little girl. But there was one very good reason to do it, and she knew it trumped nearly any excuse she could come up with, any reason she would think of. She didn't want to go back in there and admit to them that she'd do this. She was a softy, yeah, but she didn't have to seem a pushover.

Walking with more purpose, she strode into the gift shop to get the turtle she'd been looking at earlier. She'd go to Dex first thing in the morning and see if the interview had worked or not. It would probably be easier to call him, but she wanted to hand-deliver the turtle.

She hesitated outside May's door. Was she really going to do this? She wouldn't just be signing on for Phoebe but probably also for a ton of matchmaking by her well-meaning family.

She'd handle that, too, though, because she knew all her mom's tricks, and Claudia and May would be told straight out that there would be nothing more than a business arrangement between her and Dex. No hanky-panky, no kisses, no nanny-marries-the-father. Neither of those titles fit either of them anyway.

One last breath, and then she pushed through the door. May was nursing Lucinda and looked up with a smile on her face. "You're going to do it, aren't you?"

Zoe frowned. "Do you always have to steal my thunder?"

Chapter Five

The next morning, after making her deposit and ducking into the café down the street for a delicious shot of coffee, Zoe drove down tree-lined Hadley Street and pulled up in front of the sage green house owned by Dexter Zegray. May had given her directions, and Zoe had just this morning thought about not using them. But then she was reminded Phoebe had no one, and she could be someone to her. At least until Ethan came back.

Sitting in her car for a moment, she took a deep breath. All she had to do was ask him how the interview went. If it was good, then she could make up a story about something that May had wanted her to ask him, give Phoebe the turtle, and be on her way. If it hadn't gone well, then she could make her offer. Easy as a nosegay.

The house had a beautiful sun porch on the front, with flowers blossoming and waving in the early morning breeze.

And there was also the man himself, stalking back and forth across the floor-to-ceiling windows, the screens open to the early morning warmth, with Phoebe in his arms, patting her back. Zoe could hear her wails from her rolled-down windows. *Aw, man.*

She knocked on the door to the porch, then locked gazes with Dex as his heavy tread sounded on the floorboards.

He jerked the door open. "Unless you're here because you changed your mind and want to offer your babysitting services, I can't talk. I'm in the middle of something, obviously. Any offer is better than nothing at this point, as May pointed out to me. But first, take her and make it stop. Please." Dex all but thrust Phoebe into Zoe's hands.

So May had called ahead. He didn't give her a chance to say a word as he stalked to the far wall, long legs eating up the distance in seconds and broad shoulders hunched in.

Sobbing, Phoebe arched against Zoe to the point where she had to tighten her grip. She put the baby on her hip and talked to her in low tones as she handed her the turtle she'd bought at the hospital.

She took in curly brown hair and red-rimmed eyes. The baby was not a happy camper. First a bottle, then maybe a new diaper for the little girl who looked as mad as a drenched cat, her face screwed up and a fine mist of sweat coating her short hair. Hair so like Dex's. The nose was the same, too, though bright red from crying.

And then she saw the angry red welt on her forehead. She passed a soft finger over the mark before kissing Phoebe there. "What happened?"

Clapping a hand to the back of his neck, he shook his head. "I feel terrible. I turned away for one moment, and this happened."

"Let me guess. She rolled into something." As she rubbed the child's back, the wails fell to snuffling and mewling.

Dex turned around with a frown on his face. "Yes.

I'm an idiot. I placed her on the floor on a blanket, and she rolled into the coffee table." His voice deepened, and his hand squeezed until his knuckles turned white.

"It's not that big a deal, Dex. Kids have spills. Heck, the first time Justin rolled, I had him right next to me on the couch, with my hand on his belly. He rolled out from under my hand, fell off the couch, and crashed into a TV tray and got tangled in the legs. The poor guy was screaming, and I was all alone. I grabbed him, sat on the floor, and cried until Claudia heard us and came rushing up. She said the same thing I'm going to say. It happens. No permanent damage is always in the plus column."

She ran a hand down Phoebe's back and blew gently into her face. It had made Justin stop caterwauling when he was younger. And it worked this time, too.

The whole porch went dead silent. Dex's ragged breathing was the only sound filling the air. Calm, cool, always collected Dex, who did not fist his hand or fail to meet a challenge.

"You're a goddess," he whispered, staring at her as if she'd just descended from a cloud.

"No, I'm not." Though it made her neck hot to have him say so, even if it was only because she had turned off the baby alarm.

"Yes, yes, you are." He wiped his hand over his mouth, tugging his chin down. "I thought she was going to cry herself hoarse. She has a set of lungs that just won't quit."

"Why don't you go grab a bottle and take a minute to cool down? Then I can feed her. Unless you want to?"

Dex immediately put his hands behind his back. "Ah, no, she looks comfortable with you. Let's not mess with that just yet."

She took Phoebe to a wicker loveseat in the sunshine and waited. When he came in behind her a minute later, he handed her the bottle, then chose a high-backed chair far away from her, making her wonder if it was a subconscious act or one he'd knowingly made to get as far away as possible.

The baby quieted except for the noise of her sucking greedily on the bottle. As Dex continued staring at her, she fought the urge to squirm on the cushion.

Dex rubbed his hand over his hair this time before grasping the back of his neck. The way his biceps bulged momentarily distracted her. Without thinking, she let the bottle fall out of the baby's mouth, and crying began immediately. Her face flaming hot, Zoe dropped her gaze to the little girl, shushing her while returning the bottle to her waiting mouth.

The biceps went into hiding as Dex leaned forward with his elbows on his knees. "I'm going to fail at this, aren't I?"

"It really isn't that big a deal, like I said. Yes, it would be better if it doesn't happen again, but kids have accidents. They get into things. Minimal damage is what you hope for and strive for."

Shaking his head, he sat back in the chair. "So I will fail at this."

"You might want to think about baby-proofing your house. At six months she could start crawling, and you don't want her touching outlets or getting stuck under the couch."

He stood, shoving his hands into his pockets. "There are so many things to think of."

"No doubt about it, but you can do this, Dex." Justin had been a handful. So much that when Claudia moved out of their family home and into the apartment above Decadence, she'd begged Zoe to come with her. But they'd done it, and Dex was older and wiser than they'd been. He could do this, too.

He looked up at her. "Look, thanks for stopping by. I appreciate you calming her down." He crossed his arms over his chest. "We have to get back to what we were doing before the accident. I'm going through a list of people I know to see if they have any personal recommendations. The interviewing is not going well. If you'll bring her into the house, you can put her in the playpen Delly left and be on your way."

He banged into the house. He obviously expected her to follow him, but she needed a minute. Well, she had the answer to her first question. And now that left her with a choice.

Trailing along behind him, she found him in the jumble of his living room. Blankets were spread out across the floor, diapers were stacked neatly next to the coffee table that he was apparently using as a changing table. He had wipes on one end and a triple-folded towel on top of the dark wood. The whole room was filled with lots of dark wood, masculine-colored fabrics, and built-for-comfort furniture. Blues and browns ran riot over the décor, and it looked comfortable in a way she would not have pictured Dexter Zegray living. She chose the end of a worn-looking couch and settled back with Phoebe still in her arms. He chose to pace.

As Dex stared at her on his every crossing of the rug, she fought the urge to squirm again, this time on the tan couch with its old afghan and its corduroy fabric. She had meant to offer her assistance and leave quickly, since he really did need her. The little girl would nap, and Zoe could do her flower arranging then. Instead, she was lingering when she shouldn't.

"I turned around for one second and she rolled into the table. How the hell am I going to do this if one second makes a difference?" He paced some more, making her almost dizzy.

"Slow your roll, cupcake. It's really not a big deal. Of course, we don't want her to get hurt, but children can get hurt even if you're watching them at all times. They're resilient. One time, when Justin was about two, we were dancing in the living room. I was holding his hands and dancing in a circle. He let go and went straight into a wall. He was fine, had a red mark on his forehead, too, and cried like the world had come down around his ears, but it hadn't, and it won't now."

Standing with his hands on his hips, Dex eyed her from his six-foot-three height. Part of her wanted to get up and at least be a little closer to his size instead of sitting on the couch. But the baby was snuggled in tight, and she didn't want to disturb her.

"That was then, and this is now."

"And now is no different than then, not even back in the day. I'm sure babies fell out of their dresser drawers, or got caught underfoot. The trick is to do your best and hope for better."

"Is that what being a second mother to Justin taught you?"

"Yes." And being that second mother to Justin was

a downfall right now. Because, though she wanted Claudia to be happy, and she was happy her sister had finally got it right with Nate, when they'd moved she'd felt like a piece of her heart had been ripped out. She'd lived with Justin for almost eleven years, had been that second mom, and without him and Claudia in the house, it was lonely. She'd tried yoga and Zumba at her friend Jocelyn's dance studio, but you could only fill so much time with shaking your hips.

"Look, I'm not going to tell you how to run things. I'm sure you can figure it out, but I did come over to let you know that I've thought more about your offer. I can watch Phoebe during the day for you if you still need someone. She'd have to be at the shop, but I don't think that will be a problem. As you said, Justin spent many hours there, and he was never neglected. Plus, with May out with the baby, my mother is going to be back in the shop. She loves kids."

She felt like she'd been yammering, but his mouth had dropped open, and he appeared to be in shock. She couldn't even tell if he had taken a breath yet since her offer.

And then it came out as an explosive sigh.

"Please tell me you're not joking. That this is not getting back at me for whatever crime you seem to think I've committed, though you won't tell me what it is."

She scoffed at him. "I'm not that mean, and it is not a joke. You need help, I can offer help. Take it, or leave it."

"Definitely I'll take it. I don't suppose you'd consider the whole live-in nanny thing?" he asked with a cheeky smile. "It could be fun, you know."

"The smarm has to go if you want me to babysit."

"It's not smarm. It's called flirting."

"Well, you're not doing it right, so stop." She hid a smile when his lips folded in for a moment in obvious irritation.

"Fine." He tucked his hands into his pockets. "Now, let's talk money. I can give you what I was offering to the nannies, if you'd like."

"I don't need to take your money."

"You do need to take my money and be happy about it. It'll be like working two jobs at once for double the pay. Who'd pass that up?"

Obviously, she would not be, since she wasn't stupid.

"First things first, then. Let's see what you've got, and we'll make a list of what you need." She glanced down at the sleeping baby. "We can take her shopping for necessities and get that out of the way, then start this whole thing tomorrow. Does that work for you?" She looked up into his blue eyes and was taken aback at how clear they were when they weren't trying to flirt with her. Then they were just knowing in a way that irritated her. Now they were looking at her as if she were a new person.

"I think I might have underestimated you."

"Yeah, well, don't do it again, and we should be fine."

He gave a soft laugh that did things it shouldn't to her insides. She was going to have to be super-vigilant about him now. If he'd pursued her when they weren't in each other's spheres before, he might be very persistent when seeing her every day.

"Lead the way to what Delly left, and what you've

bought, and let's get started."

She placed Phoebe in the old playpen, one that probably wasn't even considered safe anymore, and asked for a pen and paper. He gave it to her, turning away after he'd delivered it as if a shock hadn't just run up her arm from where he'd brushed her fingers.

Down, girl. You are not going to make this any easier on yourself if you start lusting after the guy. He's a dog, but a dog with a baby you can help out. And that was it.

That would continue to be it for however long this whole thing took. She'd make sure of it.

****

They drove to the local super store, the radio filling in the silence. He could not, for the life of himself, believe that she was in his car. Neither could he believe that this entire thing was happening. He'd been trying for months to get her attention, and apparently all it took was a displaced baby to make her take notice. He didn't know how he felt about that—maybe more like a charity case than someone she actually wanted to spend time with.

Once he found a parking space, Zoe was quick to pull Phoebe out of the car seat, holding her as they walked in through the sliding doors. She directed Dex to get the biggest cart they had.

"Do you really think we'll need this?"

"Better safe than sorry. Do we have a budget?"

"I don't have a dollar figure in my head, but I don't want to buy too much without Ethan. When, or if, he comes back, he might have some ideas about what he wants for his daughter."

At least he hoped his brother would come back.

Ethan did as he pleased more often than not. Dex had let him because he hadn't gotten into too much trouble, and with the childhood he'd had, he deserved some freedom. But this was more than simply ditching school; this was a child who needed attention and raising. Two things he'd had no intention of ever doing again after having Ethan for the last seven years.

"Let's start on the left and make our way around." She steered the cart toward the baby section.

"I'm following your lead." And wasn't that a strange feeling?

They grabbed diapers and a changing mat, a bathtub and washcloths. A turtle towel that Zoe couldn't resist.

"I'll pay for this myself." The triangle that went over Phoebe's head was a turtle's smiling face with its tongue sticking out.

"Just put it in the basket. I can handle it." Though he didn't know how he'd feel about using it. Wasn't a normal towel good enough?

"I don't want to go over what you want to spend." She held the towel to her chest.

"It's not a problem." He grabbed the cloth and threw it into the basket.

"No, really, I can buy it. It'll be a welcome present." She made a move to take the towel out of the cart, and he swerved to thwart her.

"Just leave it. Phoebe needs things. I'll provide them. I don't know that she needs a welcome towel, or a towel at all, but I will purchase this one."

The way her eyes narrowed made him pause in his stride. Had he offended her? Angered her was more like it. She seemed to be always at the ready to do battle with him, and now that she was helping him, he couldn't seem to remove his own armor.

"Look, I'm sorry. If you want to buy the towel, you can certainly do that. This is just a lot to take in. I haven't been able to get Ethan to answer his cell phone other than the one time, and then he hung up on me before I could find out where he is. I'm overwhelmed. I shouldn't take it out on you, though."

"No, it's fine." But she took the towel out of the cart and held it tight.

What was going through that sexy mind of hers? The first time they'd met, the chemistry had been instantaneous. She'd turned him on even in a pair of athletic pants and a tank top. There'd been something about her, and then it was gone when she barely spoke to him during the whole meeting. He would have remembered if they'd met each other before, and he couldn't think of anything during the meeting itself that had turned her in those few seconds. Hell, he even continued to send flowers from her shop, hoping she'd finally unbend enough to talk to him. But it hadn't happened yet, at least not until he brought Phoebe into the picture.

He felt Phoebe grab his finger and stared down at her. She was so little, her dark hair curly like his was when he was young and her bright blue eyes focused right on him as she tried to shove his finger into her mouth.

Then Zoe was there with a pacifier and a crumpled package she threw into the cart. "That you can pay for."

"What else?" Dex wheeled the cart down yet another aisle, trying not to be overwhelmed by the sheer amount of things available for children. They had their own tubs and special towels and bibs and bottles and onesies and blankets with bear heads... It was too much.

At this rate he'd have nightmares about being buried alive under a mountain of stuffed bears. Or make that turtles, since the little girl seemed to have an affinity for the hard-shelled animal. Every time they passed one she pointed and grunted. Zoe had put one in the cart with her, stopping the grunting only until she saw the next one. So then they had to get her a rubber turtle for the tub and another towel with a turtle on the head. He only hoped his credit card could handle all this and that Ethan was going to be willing to work his ass off when he came home, to pay the bill back.

"I think we're almost done," Zoe finally said as they rounded yet another corner into an aisle teetering with stacks of more diapers. She checked the list she'd made and crossed out another item.

He pulled his own list out of his front pocket. They'd gathered the few meager things on his after about five minutes. Thank God he'd brought her along. What would he have done without a thermometer for the child's ear or one of those bulb suction things to get the snot out of her nose? "To be honest, I would have been done about thirty minutes ago."

Zoe stopped in the middle of the aisle with those graceful hands on those full hips. He looked back into her eyes, because it was the safest place at this point, though they were an intriguing hazel when she was about to go off on him.

"Everything we got is a necessity."

He pulled a package of twelve bibs from the cart. "All these?"

She grabbed the package out of his hand and tossed it back into the cart behind Phoebe. "Yes, all those. She is definitely going to need every single one of those bibs. You have a drooler on your hands, Dexter Zegray."

As if to prove her point, Phoebe smiled a wet grin, and Zoe laughed.

Chapter Six

"I'm going to need some things for my place, too. I'll pay for them, since I'm sure I'll use them as honorary auntie to May's new daughter." She separated a few things from the rest in a pile at the back of the cart.

"I'll pay for them," he snapped.

"No need to get testy. If you want to pay for them, go for it. I know you're made of money. I was just trying to save you some so that maybe you'll come back to my flower shop for your many bouquets." She shot him a look that should have scorched his eyebrows, but he just raised one of those brows at her.

"I haven't been sending any bouquets at all, and I'm certainly not cheating on you with another florist. I know you're the best in town."

"Well, that's something, I guess."

"And I'm not made of money. Those bouquets are—"

"Yeah, let's not talk about that when we're having such a good time with Phoebe. Your playboy activities are none of my business unless you take that business elsewhere. "

She shot down the aisle and over to the next before he could tell her anything more. Picking out an inexpensive but good playpen, she chose two, added one changing table, and leaned all three items against the shelving for him to put in the basket. There were some things she did not need at her place.

He caught up with her, but she kept on moving ahead. Ready for the shopping trip to be over at this point. She'd done her duty and was ready to go home. She'd spent enough time out this morning and needed to get back to work. Being away for so long could get her into hot water if orders started piling in, or if someone needed an emergency flower arrangement for an "I'm sorry" or something to let a special person know they wanted them to get well soon.

Silence reigned on the walk out of the store after Dex slid his credit card and took the receipt that was longer than his entire arm.

She left him to buckle Phoebe into her seat in the back and flipped through the messages on her phone. She hadn't expected to be gone this long and was now raring to get back to her last day of freedom for the next little while.

"I'll help you carry everything in, and we can transfer the things for my place to my car, and then I have to get going. I have orders stacking up and need to get back."

She got no argument from him and was surprised when he started the car and simply drove, turning the radio up a bit but not too much. He drove along, looking in the rearview mirror that reflected into the mirror they'd installed in the back seat so he could look at Phoebe whenever he needed to.

His face was so serious; she was used to seeing him smiling and laughing. This was not the Dex she knew, but another, more staid man who had taken his place now that Phoebe had come into his life. Was this the real Dex?

She might never know, and she'd never ask because that would invite conversation she didn't want.

While she'd been looking at his profile, he turned down a road that would most certainly not be taking them back to her flower shop.

"Where are we going?"

"I have a quick errand to run. Since it's on our way, I thought I could do it before going back into town. It'll only take a moment."

Wasn't that what all men said?

Well, she'd just stay in the car with Phoebe while he ran his errand. Surely by now the little girl might need a second diaper change. Zoe had changed her in the store, but that didn't mean the little stinker wasn't in need. And she could probably use another bottle. Something Zoe had thought to throw in the bag when Dex was ready to walk out the door.

It didn't take him long to run into the hardware store and come back out, but it was enough time for Zoe to realize that if she was going to be working with him as the nanny, she needed to change her attitude. Out of all the casual dating she'd done, no one had been very important to her. The fact that each of them had married the woman right after her was a running joke at this point, since it was good for business.

She wasn't going to admit that Dex got under her skin far more than any of the others had, especially since she'd never even dated him. However, if they were going to continue to be in each other's space over the next few weeks, at least, then she needed to get her head right. And that started with an apology.

"Sorry for coming off short," she said when he

returned to the car. "There's no excuse, so I'm not going to make one up. Let's just keep Phoebe at the center of this whole thing, and it should all work out fine."

With one hand on the steering wheel, he looked at her in a way that made her vaguely uncomfortable. Not in a bad way, but in a way that made her wish he was about to seduce her, not forgive her for being bitchy.

"No worries. Phoebe is the main concern here. As long as we both keep the focus there, I'm sure we'll get along fine." He started the car. "Home, then? I know you have a lot of stuff to do at the shop, and we've kept you long enough."

"Yes, please."

The drive wasn't a long one, but it felt like forever. Should she have said more? Let him off the hook easier? What he did and who he did it with were none of her concern. Tons of other guys had flirted with her, and it had all been harmless fun. What was the difference here?

She wasn't willing to explore that at the moment.

When the car came to a stop in Dex's driveway, she turned to him, only to have his lips land on hers. He pulled back after a moment that didn't last long enough.

"Sorry, I was aiming for your cheek, to say thank you." His face was serious, again, and she just couldn't stand it.

Grabbing his ears, she pulled him in for a real kiss. She knew it wouldn't go anywhere and had no intention of pursuing something with a man who had a different flavor every week, but his lips were too tempting not to get a real taste, since she'd never have one again.

Playing with fire was an understatement.

Out in front of his house, she let his lips possess hers, his hands cradle the back of her head, and the console dig into her rib cage. His kiss was magic, a perfect blend of sweet and hard, tongues dueling and teeth nibbling. She knew from the first moment she'd seen him that he would be good at this. It was one of the many reasons she had labeled him MAN with all caps before she'd realized who he was.

She really should pull back, but she stayed for one last nip of his teeth on her bottom lip. If what he'd said earlier was true, he was going to regret this and not want to do it again, because he had Phoebe to think about. She'd be off the hook and have something to dream about tonight, at least.

"Phew," he said with his forehead against hers. His breath whispered over her slightly swollen lips and made her flutter inside. This close she could see flecks of green in his eyes and wondered how someone so perfect could be so wrong for her.

Then again, who was she to complain? He did nothing more than she did—casually date. Though she didn't date as often as he seemed to. It was semantics. And a part of her realized that she did not want to be one in a long string of ladies. For once she wanted to be special, and he would never give that to her.

"That can't happen again." She gathered her purse, looking him straight in the eyes.

"I don't know if my heart could take it. You are one great kisser, Zoe Bradley. I can't do this, though. I can't give you anything while I have Phoebe. I really wish we would have explored that more when I was free to do so."

Yeah, her too. Instead of saying that, she got out of

the car, opened the back door, kissed Phoebe on the head and waved goodbye without helping him take anything into the house. Her heart might have been palpitating in her chest, but she would be damned before she showed that to Casanova.

****

Ethan's cell rang and rang. Where in the world could he be, and why wouldn't he pick up the phone? Dex was torn between fear that he really wasn't okay and anger over the way he was avoiding his responsibilities. This was not Dex's child, and yet here he was the one fully responsible. Again.

Dropping Zoe off this afternoon had been torture. At least she had texted to say she would still watch Phoebe. He was making mistakes left and right at this point, but taking Zoe to bed as a continuation of that incredible kiss, knowing he couldn't do more than that, would have been the worst. She deserved more than the few moments here and there he might be able to spare around running his life, this house, and raising a little girl.

He rested his forehead against his bedroom wall with his cell phone to his ear for the tenth time, hoping Ethan would be so irritated he'd just pick up the phone to get it to stop ringing. The call went right to voice mail this time.

"Ethan, it's Dex. Fine. I get it. You think you need time and distance to figure out what you're going to do. But I get stuck with the issue in the meantime, man. This isn't just about you. You have a kid here I don't know anything about. Call me. Now. You'd better not be out there somewhere hurt."

He punched the End Call button. Where was his

brother? He'd been mad before, stalked off before, but Dex had never known him to completely disappear.

Thank God for Zoe. He had never been more thankful for a helping hand. When his parents died he'd done everything himself, but Ethan had been twelve, not a six-month-old little girl.

His phone chimed in his hand, bringing him out of his thoughts to read the new text: *I'm fine. I can't think right now. Give me time.*

He needed time to think? A baby was not a thing you could decide to take on or not. Especially not your own child. If nothing else, Dex knew he had raised Ethan better than that. They'd often talked about taking responsibility for your actions. That there were things in life that had to be taken care of. A baby was one of those things. When had Ethan abandoned all he'd learned? Everything Dex had taught him? Everything they, as a pair of survivors, stood for?

But Dex held himself back from shooting off a text before he'd had time to think through his response. Saying the wrong thing now could keep Ethan from coming back at all. There was too much at stake to not think before he acted. And now, with Zoe's help, he felt more settled. He might not know her very well, since initially it was just lust propelling him on, but on a gut level he knew enough to trust in her ability to care for Phoebe better than he could by himself. Hell, probably anyone in the world knew more about babies than he did, but Zoe seemed to be a natural.

His plan had been to get Ethan on his feet and then go have the life he'd never gotten to have in his twenties. Some dating, some flirting, some free time without a care in the world but for himself. Nothing that would jeopardize his livelihood or his life, but for years he'd looked forward to having the ability and the freedom to blow off some steam without an impressionable teenager under foot. An end to the restrictions he'd put on himself to make sure he set a good example, without his parents to guide Ethan. He'd looked forward to doing all those things he'd never done while trying to make a living and a home for his brother.

But now he had to make a home for another child, one he knew nothing about. A least with Ethan he'd had six years before he'd left for college, and at twelve his brother had been old enough to do some things for himself. This little girl needed everything done for her. He didn't think he was up to the task—with or without Zoe's help.

His hands were sweating and his heart racing. She was so tiny. Why was he so scared?

Because she was so tiny, he finally admitted. Give him a rough-and-tumble boy, and he was good. He'd sponsored several Little League baseball teams through his law practice and had played some ball with them, talked with them at their awards dinners. But he'd never been responsible for them, and they were all capable of taking care of themselves to some extent. Even Ethan had been old enough to make his own meals when their parents had died. As a child of alcoholics, if he didn't make it, he didn't eat. Dex remembered that too well.

But not so with Phoebe, and that was making him shake in his socks. He was not going to be okay, and if the child slept through the night, he'd be astounded.

After putting in another call to Ethan, Dex headed upstairs with his baby monitor and the big box of cubby cabinet wood. He listened for Phoebe, who was still downstairs safely tucked in the new playpen in the family room, trying to be silent with the hammer. Never once did she wake up, even when he went back downstairs to make sure she was still breathing. Satisfied that her chest rose and fell in the right kind of rhythm, he finished the cubbies in record time, pleased with the way the cloth drawers in all the colors of the rainbow looked. Zoe had assured him the different drawers would work well. And she was right.

Very carefully he picked up Phoebe from the playpen, where she had been supported by stuffed animals and surrounded by more stuffed animals while he was upstairs. He should get the crib put together, but right now that was a worry for another time. At this point, he just wanted to fall into bed and get a good night's rest. He had a lot of work, both personal and professional, in front of him. And he'd be doing the majority of it himself. Thank God for Zoe, or he might have joined Phoebe in her cry fest that morning.

****

Tuesday started a heck of a lot earlier than Dex was used to when crying in the dark woke him. It took him a moment to remember where he was and why on earth there would be a crying baby anywhere in his vicinity.

It came crashing back soon enough when the wailing escalated. He threw his legs over the edge of the bed and stumbled against the new cubby holder to find the end table light.

Squinting against the dim glow, he tried not to stumble on anything else. Crashing into the side of the playpen would not be a good idea. He did stub his toe on the edge of his bed, trying to avoid something shadowed on the floor that turned out to be a stuffed animal.

Scooping up Phoebe, he made the same noises Zoe had made yesterday afternoon. Did babies normally cry this much and with this much force? He had no idea, and, though he'd intended to read that *Babies for Dummies* book before lying down last night, he'd ended up falling into bed after putting Phoebe into her playpen.

On the way downstairs, he checked her diaper as Zoe had taught him but felt no squishiness. At the landing, the crying became mewling as she rubbed her forehead against his bare chest. Poor thing. Poor him— it was four in the morning, according to the hall clock.

Grabbing from the refrigerator a bottle he'd mixed earlier, he shook it a few times, then popped it into the microwave for thirty seconds instead of fifteen. He shook it again, then tested it on his wrist. Perfectly warm.

As perfectly warm as the little girl felt against his chest. She made a pitiful cry as he walked into the living room and settled into the couch. Maybe he should think about just staying down here for the next few nights until he got this bottle thing down.

But he needed room to stretch out, and he supposed she did, too. Propping Phoebe up on his arm, he tucked her in close and put the bottle into her searching mouth. She immediately latched on like a starving puppy.

Her slurping and sucking were the only sounds at four in the morning in his too-quiet house. Ethan's music should be playing upstairs, a murmur down the hall that told Dex his brother was here, under his roof, and okay.

He'd listened to that sound for years now. They'd fought over how loud it had been in his early teens. Ethan's tastes hadn't changed, he still went for hard rock, but the volume had toned down until it had become a backdrop, one Dex missed.

He thought about grabbing his phone and calling Ethan just to see if he could catch him off guard enough to actually answer the phone. God only knew where the boy was, or if he was sleeping in anything other than his car.

Halfway through the bottle, Dex burped Phoebe with a towel he found on the coffee table from an earlier feeding. Somewhere in that jumble of things Zoe had bought today was something she'd called a burpee rag, but a towel would do just fine. He threw the dark blue material over his shoulder and brought her up. She stirred, her fingers scrabbling at the back of his neck when she let out a belch that would have made a trucker proud.

She startled a laugh out of him, which in turn startled a cry out of her. He quickly got himself under control, tucking her back into his arm and putting the bottle into her mouth again. This was one hungry little girl.

But, as with the bottle he'd watched Zoe feed her before, Phoebe fell fast asleep with about an ounce remaining. He wasn't going to risk burping her again.

He did, however, sit for just a couple of minutes and look down at a face that was so like a feminine version of Ethan when he was tiny. Dex hadn't had much to do with the infant Ethan, but he remembered being happy to be a big brother even if he was too cool to admit it to his friends.

Now he was an uncle. Dex sighed, his head back against the top of the couch. An uncle who was in charge of a tiny person he had no idea how to care for. Though he had to admit he hadn't done too badly so far.

Stretching out on the couch, he put her in between his stomach and the corduroy back, then watched her chest rise and fall. She needed him, and somehow he'd figure this out. Tomorrow morning, though, he should make a doctor's appointment for her. He needed to see about how healthy and normal she was in the scheme of things. It had been bugging him all day. Delly had left without more than two words, and that wailing scared him.

Delly Ferndale. He thought about the bouncy girl with the quiet laughter. She'd been damaged in her own way with a potentially abusive mother, but she'd been good for Ethan, a balance to his sometimes irritating mood swings. She had worked on getting him to go back to counseling about his parents' death and had looked to Dex to help convince him. Dex had told her Ethan was capable of making his own decisions. Mainly because Dex refused to do any grieving of his own beyond what was in the past and would not force Ethan to do something he himself was not willing to do.

She and Ethan had continued dating for months, and then she'd just left one day, not leaving a forwarding address or even giving Ethan a reason for dumping him. Maybe this bundle tucked up against him was the reason.

Maybe she'd left when she found out she was pregnant. He only hoped she had taken good care of herself while she'd been gone, and had given Phoebe everything she physically needed. He would face whatever might come, but having a new baby with health problems would not make things easier. He'd still do it, because that was the way he was built, but he'd need support. As evidenced so far, he wasn't good at asking.

He'd deal with that if it happened. No use borrowing trouble when he had enough on his hands right now. Delly had left it on his doorstep.

Talking about it today with Zoe had made him wonder at the circumstances and the timing. Had Delly had enough? Thought that she might harm the baby if she kept her? Had she thought she couldn't provide a good life for the little girl and wanted to give her to her father instead of up for adoption?

These were all questions he was probably never going to have answers to. But he did need answers from Ethan.

He drifted off after another moment, worried that Ethan wouldn't find his way back home anytime soon, and Dex would be stuck all by himself, again.

Chapter Seven

When Dex didn't show up at eight a.m. the next day, Zoe was concerned. Then again, maybe it was just taking longer to get out the door with the baby than Dex had anticipated. She let it go as she dug into making sure her list of table arrangements for the Harlow family's fiftieth anniversary party was as complete as possible.

At nine, she called, but no one answered. She waved a quick goodbye to Claudia, telling her to man the phones, and headed over to Dex's. And now she was standing at his side door, not sure what to do. She could use the key he'd given her yesterday, but she'd hate to intrude if he didn't want her there. Maybe Ethan had come home and they were talking, needing no interruptions.

But she didn't see any other cars in the drive and was certain Ethan had a car. Key in hand, she hesitated. Maybe she should check the driveway behind the house first. She'd be utterly embarrassed if she walked into Dex's house uninvited only to find he was gone.

The big brown, double barn doors of the garage were firmly secured with a padlock and not a single peep came from inside. A peek through the window showed only his SUV, so she turned back to the house. Now or never, then.

The key turned easily in the lock. She kept hold of

the knob as she moved it clockwise to make as little noise as possible. If Phoebe was asleep, Zoe didn't want to be the one to wake her. She made her way through the house quietly, softly calling Dex's name.

They weren't in the kitchen. From the window, she looked onto the deck just in case they were taking in some of the beautiful late May sun. The house was silent and so was the deck. She turned to rest against the counter to decide if she really wanted to go upstairs to Dex's room, and that was when she spotted a broad back lying horizontally on the couch she'd sat on yesterday.

She tiptoed into the living room. She'd just check on them, then leave as quietly as she'd come. Once they woke up, Dex could bring the baby.

Dex's big body was in a C shape on the couch, his back to the room and his knees drawn up to make a nest for a peacefully sleeping Phoebe. As she watched, both of their chests rose and fell in unison. His hair was mussed, and his long lashes fanned out on his cheeks. He looked younger, less worried, as he slept.

And she should not be staring at him.

She should leave. Now that she knew they were both fine, she should leave and let Dex come to her when he was ready. As she moved away, it was as if Phoebe sensed her presence. The baby's beautiful, long lashes lifted, and a smile broke out on her face as she reached for Zoe.

The wall of resolve to leave and let Dex come to her on his own wavered as Zoe moved around to the back of the couch and leaned over to pick Phoebe up. Dex stirred, then jerked awake as soon as Zoe had the baby in her arms. Their eyes connected, his sleepy and hers wide open as he sent her a smile that made the walls a bit shaky.

His yawn was so huge she saw his back molars. To divert her attention, her gaze dropped down to the hand he'd put above his heart. She quickly looked away from that, too, staring down at the baby so she didn't ogle his bare chest. Ogling was not good for their working relationship.

"What time is it?" he said around another yawn.

Looking at her wristwatch, she relayed the time and stumbled back as he jumped off the sofa.

"Oh, man, I'm late. I'm late."

"You sound like the White Rabbit." She snickered while tickling Phoebe's tummy.

"Does that make you Alice or the Cheshire Cat?"

"I'm thinking Alice, since I feel like I've dropped into a rabbit hole."

He dragged a hand down his face and yawned again. "Right. It's an apt description at this point. Although I think I might be Alice in this one."

She looked him up and down, lingering on parts she shouldn't. "I'm thinking you're more of an Alec than an Alice."

He stared at her for a second, then started laughing. The laughing crinkled his eyes and made him far more attractive than he should be. She did not have the time or the inclination to find him appealing, she told herself, even as her stomach fluttered in a way it hadn't in years. He'd made the rules clear, and she'd be dumb to forget that. There was also the pickle jar loosener thing to consider. He might not want to be with her, but if he found someone else, she did not want to make his wedding flowers.

"Anyway, are you ready for me to take Phoebe with me?"

He stretched, and she really wished he'd put on a shirt. "If you don't mind. That way I can get a shower before I get started."

And that was just one more image she did not need.

She focused on gathering everything she might need at the shop as quickly as she could, then made a beeline for the door, all while trying not to look at his lightly haired chest.

"So I'll drop her back off at four?"

"Sure." He brushed by her, his arm lightly tapping hers as he smiled at her. She willed her knees to absolutely not go weak.

As he walked up the stairs, she double-checked all her supplies and packed up the blankets and bottles. The diaper bag had every single thing she could think of and a few extra things just in case. This would be the first day she had the little girl at the shop for more than an hour while it was open. She had no idea how it was going to go, but she wanted to be as prepared as possible.

Ten minutes later they were on the road. Dex had not come out of the shower yet, but Zoe wasn't sure she wanted to be there when he did. There was something about him that drew her, and he did not want her to be drawn. The way he'd agreed they couldn't kiss anymore was proof of that.

Pulling up at the back door, she strategized how best to get everything into the shop and where exactly to put it all. She had to make sure there was ample room for Phoebe to breathe, but also not hinder the customers who came in to order any number of things

Decadence sold.

In the end, she didn't have to think too much because Claudia knocked on her window before she could even shut off the car.

"Is the sweetie-cheeks here? Oh, there she is, in the back. Doesn't she look adorable?"

Zoe thought she looked pretty cute, too. She'd dressed her in a yellow-and-white-checked one-piece outfit with a huge smiling sunflower on her belly.

Claudia had Phoebe unstrapped from the car seat and was cooing to her within seconds. She took the baby into the shop without a backward glance, leaving Zoe standing next to the car in a huff. She was going to have to carry everything else in by herself. It figured.

When she finally lugged it all in, Claudia was showing Phoebe all the files and folders on the desk, pointing out pictures of flowers and weddings on the wall, and telling her that someday that would be her.

Zoe let Claudia have her fun before the next meeting, scheduled at ten, for a graduation party. Tuesday mornings were set aside for shop-wide meetings, too, but there might not be much to discuss at this point, with May out.

The day got rolling, and it spun by as fast as a tornado, but with less destruction. Zoe spent a lot of time explaining who the baby was, which also gave her the opportunity to talk more with anyone who came in, even if it wasn't for her flowers. Perhaps business would pick up even more.

Phoebe napped in the back room, snoozing away with a little snore every once in a while that made Zoe smile while she worked on the accounts.

Things went seamlessly; Phoebe was fed and

played with by many of the people who came in and out throughout the day. Zoe had been right that Phoebe would fit in with her work schedule. Everyone took turns, and it was like having Justin there all over again.

Around three that afternoon, Dex called to see how Phoebe was doing. They chatted for a few moments until he said he had a favor to ask.

"What's up?"

"I don't want to impose."

"Dex, I'll let you know if I think it's an imposition. Now spill."

"Well, I have a client who's running a few minutes late and told me that the documents she drew up are going to be more extensive than she first led me to believe. Is there any way you can keep Phoebe a little bit longer? I hate to ask on the first day, but I don't want to turn this woman away."

"It's not a problem. Take as long as you need to." It wasn't like she was doing anything tonight.

"I'll bring dinner to make up for it."

She almost declined, since it might be more than she could handle. It was one thing to lust after a guy and know he couldn't be yours, but to continue to throw yourself into situations where the feelings were just going to ratchet up was not her scene.

However, dinner would be nice. And she was perfectly capable of keeping her hands and her thoughts to herself. Even after that kiss.

"Sounds good. We'll be waiting for you."

"Six at the latest."

"Six, got it," she said before hanging up and putting her phone back in her pocket.

When she turned around, Claudia and Mona, her

72

mom, were both standing there staring at her. "What, do I have something on my face?"

"Nothing but a grin that says more than you would think," Claudia said.

Mona just smiled and folded her hands at her waist.

"I do not have a grin that says anything." She tried to control her facial muscles into a frown. Unfortunately, it wasn't working.

"You definitely have a grin, dear, no matter how much you try to disguise it. And from your demeanor on the phone, I'm guessing one Dexter Zegray put it there."

"Dex did not put anything anywhere on me." Lord, that sounded pathetic and was only going to fuel the fire she could see burning at the surface of the two women's curiosity. She'd have to diffuse this now, or they would never let it go and would see innuendo and double meanings behind every single thing that happened while Zoe watched Phoebe. "Look, I am watching his niece, and we're having a great working relationship. He doesn't want complications, and I don't want complications, so we're good."

Mona took the piece of cloth that was draped over her shoulder and swatted at Zoe with it. "It could be more, you know. He's hunky, and look what he's doing, taking in this baby girl. You could do worse, and you know it."

Zoe could list at least twelve men she had done worse with, but her mother wouldn't listen to that excuse. Better to go with the bare facts. "He has Phoebe to concentrate on, and he was very specific that he couldn't do any kind of relationship while everything was up in the air with her."

Claudia pounced on that like it was a ball of catnip and she the frisky cat. "So the two of you have talked about seeing each other? I like the sound of that."

Zoe blew out a breath, aware she had laid that trap for herself and walked right into it. "It doesn't matter how the conversation came about. What matters is that Dex is certain he wants no part of dating for a long, long while." To be honest, it had sounded to her like maybe until Phoebe grew up. And that was fine with her, since it kept him off limits no matter how much she wanted another one of those kisses, despite how much of a playboy she thought he was.

Although, Zoe couldn't exactly understand not dating just because you had a kid. It was very possible to date and have kids. People had successfully done it for years and years. But the fact was that if he didn't want to date her then she wouldn't open the door for some other woman to swoop in and get him straight to the altar, as she had with the other twelve men. Which was fine with her.

The first one she didn't even allow herself to think about because he was the one who had set her on this path in the first place. He was the one she hadn't even told Claudia the complete truth about, and she wasn't about to go there with her mom.

"Now can we drop this, please, so we can move on to other things? I have bouquets to make and ribbons to tie. I'm sure you all have things to do too."

"Fine, fine. I don't know why you have to take all the fun out of this. You were having a grand old time when I was falling for Nate. I think it's only fair that I get to razz you about a new beau."

"When I have a new beau you are more than

welcome to razz away. Since what I currently have is a business relationship, I think it's best not to go there."

Claudia and Mona exchanged a look that Zoe pointedly ignored. There was no need to tell them that, less than a day ago, Dex had almost kissed the panties right off her. And she would have liked it, too. That kiss could have been a prelude to something more. Playboy or not, she was almost sorry it hadn't gone any farther.

But she knew in the end it wouldn't work out. Normally that was fine with her; in fact, it was the way she lived her life—no strings, no commitments, just fun. But something told her Dex might have a chance of breaking through that rut and dragging her into territory she wasn't ready to explore yet.

She had been serious all those months ago when she told Claudia she only wanted fun right now. There was plenty of time to settle down later. And at this point, she finally had a home of her own, the business she loved, and a little girl to spoil. It was enough. It had to be.

Chapter Eight

Dex loosened his tie as he carried out the food he'd ordered from Joey's Pizzeria. Thankfully, the girl at the front counter knew Zoe well and was able to tell him what to order.

He was ten minutes late to her house. Balancing all the food, he knocked on the back door on the outside of the building. He'd never been to her place before. Hell, he'd never been this close to her for this amount of time, ever.

And he couldn't think like that now, or he would completely derail himself from his promise to Phoebe that he would take care of her. It had worked with Ethan—well to some extent, this incident notwithstanding—and it would work again, even if Ethan never came back.

That thought gave him a feeling akin to heartburn, so he put it away and waited for Zoe to answer his knock.

When she did, his system went on overdrive. He should have remembered what seeing her could do to his libido. *Man, I didn't think this whole thing through. I should have just asked her to meet me at the restaurant. That or gotten her dinner and then left with the baby and my dinner.*

Her lips were rosy, her oval face shone, and the smile on those lips was enough to make him hope his knees would hold. What was it about her that made him like this? He'd never been more than a casual dater, when he did actually date after Ethan had graduated. In over a year, he'd never met someone who made him want to be better than he was, and yet here she was, and completely out of reach because of the baby cradled in her arms.

A moment had passed, but in it was an awkwardness he couldn't afford to have in this business relationship. She was still smiling at him even though her forehead had crinkled together. Before she could ask what was wrong, he found his tongue.

"Hey, it's a good thing the lady down at Joey's knew you, or I would have totally messed up your order."

She laughed and stepped back so he could enter her domain. He'd never been here, but a single glance told him it was all her. The colors were bold, the furniture comfortable and arranged in a way that showed him she was an artist outside the flower shop, too.

"Oh, man, tell me you got me a California Cheesesteak, hold the onions and the oregano."

"None other." And the equilibrium was back, putting him on solid ground again.

"Come on into the kitchen, and we'll set things out."

"I got paper plates so we wouldn't have a mess to clean up. I didn't want to make more work for you when you've already pulled a double shift."

"Thanks." She looked at him through lowered lashes, and he didn't know what to do with his hands. Thankfully they were filled with delicious-smelling Italian food.

When she went to take the boxes from him, he told her to show him the way. He wasn't ready to hold Phoebe just yet, and he knew she'd hand the baby over once his hands were empty. She'd done it before. Frankly, it had been nice to be away from her for the whole day. And while that made him a bad person, he couldn't help but be honest with himself.

Phoebe went into the carrier on the kitchen table, with the turtle she hadn't let go of since Zoe had handed it to her. The baby waved it around and made little squeaks while Zoe smiled at her and tickled her stomach.

Dex turned away to put the food on the counter and begin dividing things out. He'd gotten lasagna for himself, with a small side salad and bread. He wanted to drag out dinner if he could. Maybe if he took long enough, Phoebe would fall asleep on the way home and sleep through the night. He couldn't think of a better way for this day to end.

Sitting across from Zoe wasn't bad, either, but he was trying hard not to think about that.

"So how was your day?" she asked as she placed their plates on the table and got silverware out of the drawer next to the sink.

He shifted in his chair at the domesticity of the moment. He didn't want this, and wouldn't for years to come, now.

Clearing his throat, he used his fork to cut his lasagna, to give it a chance to cool down. "Good. I have several new contracts and several closed out. Your Uncle Al says hi, by the way, and wants me to thank you and perhaps buy you some kind of extravagant present—his words—for saving his bacon by letting me come back to work."

"He's such a teddy bear." She unwrapped her sandwich and broke the two halves apart. Sticking a napkin on her lap, she leaned forward and dug in.

He'd never liked those women who would order a small salad and nibble on a single leaf for the whole dinner. He liked women who ate and had curves. Zoe had it all, plus some.

And he absolutely needed to stop thinking like that if he had any hope of surviving the next few weeks. "How was your day?"

"Actually, it went really well. Phoebe was a peach all day, and people adored her when they came in the store. I forgot what fun it can be to have a little one around." She smiled, but there was something a little sad in her eyes.

It would be best if he didn't ask about it. It really would. However, despite his best intentions, he couldn't stop himself.

"Do you miss having Claudia and Justin around?"

The smile turned sadder yet, drooping at the corners. "You know, with everything going on and everyone so happy with their babies and their new relationships, not a single person has asked me that." She looked down at her sandwich and toyed with a piece of tomato. "Not that I want them to be anything but happy, but yes, I miss them. Justin was like a son to me, and it's weird here without them. Without him tromping down the hall, his voice cracking, without Claudia making bread or her homemade lasagna that would put your dinner to shame. Not that Joey's isn't awesome, but Claudia has this special ingredient..." She blew out a breath. "I do miss them a lot. I get to see them, but I'm not a part of their home life like I used to be, and it hurts."

Again, against his best intentions, he placed a hand over hers. "I'm sorry."

"Thanks. It's nothing to complain about. Claudia and Justin have the family they always should have had, and after trying for so many years Brad and May have their baby. Have you seen her?"

"I did today, actually. I went by during my lunch. Thanks again for sending the bouquet. She loved it."

Zoe laughed. "Of course she did. I made it."

He chuckled with her and squeezed her hand, then let it go reluctantly. "We should get out of your hair."

She shook her head, sending her blond ponytail waving. "Since we are on the subject of how things are going... Have you gotten hold of Ethan yet?"

He tried hard not to shutter down at the question. She had spilled to him about Claudia and Justin when she didn't have to, and she was part of this. She might not have a stake in it like he did, but the sooner Ethan came home, the sooner she could get back to her own life. "Unfortunately, no. He isn't picking up his phone, and the last time I talked to him, he hung up on me."

"Yikes, that's got to be frustrating."

"That about covers it. I raised him better than this."

"Wait." Zoe stopped with her sandwich halfway to her mouth. She put it down with a thump. "*You* raised him?"

She didn't know. Great, now he was going to have to explain. Although if there was anyone in this town besides Brad or Sam who wouldn't judge, he knew it was Zoe.

"You want the short version or the sordid one?" he

asked in all seriousness.

This time it was she who reached out for his hand. "As much as you want to give me."

In that moment he knew he'd like to give her his all, but the baby in the carrier sitting to his left made that impossible. Instead, he would trust her with the truth, then let it speak for itself.

Turning his palm up, he entwined their fingers. "When I was young I couldn't wait to get out of the house. My parents were drunks and should never have had children." He paused and swallowed. "As soon as I could, I left for college. Ethan was six to my eighteen, but I didn't think about anything more than getting the hell away as soon as possible. Ethan won't talk much about those years, but when he turned twelve they died in a single-car accident on the way home from a bar. Ethan was home alone. He was the one who answered the door when the cops came to report the deaths."

She gripped his fingers hard. Somehow that made it easier to continue.

"I was called, and I left my criminal class in the middle of a final to come get him. Funny how I remember that so clearly. I had finished the nineteenth question and only had four more to go. I was feeling good about my mini-essays, and then I was called to the office immediately on the classroom phone. I had no idea what for, but I could tell it was going to be something big."

The last half of her sandwich sat untouched in front of her. He didn't want her food to go cold, but he also didn't want to give up the warmth of her hand.

"So I gunned it home and found this kid who I knew almost nothing about, sitting in his room and staring at a wall covered in video-game posters. I didn't even know what to say to him when he turned to me, looked me up and down, and said, 'If you're going to take me to foster care, let's get it over with.' I about had a fit."

"I can't even imagine."

"Apparently our parents had been threatening to turn him over every time he did anything that rocked their little drunken ship, like needing them to come in for parent-teacher conferences or a band concert."

"I don't know what to say." A tear glistened in her eye and he wanted to wipe it away, but that felt more intimate than the kiss they'd shared in his car.

He blew out a breath. "Anyway, I took him back to school with me, got a job, kept up with my school work, and got him and myself to graduation. It took a little longer than I had anticipated, but we did it. I fought over and over again in court to keep custody of him and did everything and anything I had to in order to keep him out of the system. When he started getting in trouble in his junior year, we talked and we moved here to start over again. I really thought we were on the road to good stuff. And now this."

"But this can be good, too, Dex. I know it doesn't look that way now, but you're good with her, and Ethan will come back. With a story like that, he has to come back for his daughter. He might not have the same drive as you do, but knowing what you sacrificed for him and how you fought for him will bring him back. I know it."

"I hope you're right."

"I'm always right," she said with a grin.

And he couldn't fight the impulse he had to kiss her. Instead of leaning over the table, though, and having a retake of the way they'd almost gotten out of control against his car, he simply kissed the back of her hand while staring straight into her eyes. "I wish things were different."

"But they're not, and she needs you. Ethan is going to need you, too. I get that. It wasn't easy being the younger one in the house with a pregnant teenaged older sister. There was a lot of fighting and side-choosing, and I always came down on Claudia's side. It's one of the reasons we moved out together to raise Justin. He didn't need that tension. And I never hesitated to do my share. You won't hesitate to do yours. And Ethan will come back because he knows from your example that you have to do the right thing, not just the easy thing."

"I appreciate that," he said and kissed the back of her hand again before resting their joined hands back on the table.

She looked at the way their fingers entwined, then looked up at him directly. "Why do you have to be so damn nice, Dex? And why the hell couldn't I have seen it before?"

He had no answer, but he had the same regrets. Although how much harder would this have been if he and Zoe were dating and he had to cut it off to take care of Phoebe? Infinitely harder. Astronomically harder, and that would have just been the letting-go part. Staying away would have been damn near impossible.

"Anyway," she said brightly as her eyes shone with what were most likely unshed tears, "Phoebe was great today, and I look forward to having her tomorrow. Do you think you might need a longer day again? I have Zumba in the evening, but I can cancel if need be."

She was attempting to get them off the subject, he knew that, but his brain wouldn't disengage from thoughts of them being together. He cleared his throat and told his brain to knock it the hell off. "Ah, no, Zumba is fine. I don't want to inconvenience you in any way. I appreciate the offer, though, and guess I'd better ask you to make a list of those extravagant presents for me to pick from."

"You don't have to buy me anything." She laughed and shook her head. "I'm perfectly happy to help out."

"Thanks." And then they talked about inconsequential things, giving him a moment to collect himself and then thank her for taking care of Phoebe for the day. By the time he left it was eight o'clock. Phoebe was fed, changed into her pajamas, and nodding off as he headed out the door to his car.

All in all, it had been a good day, something he hadn't thought he'd have for a while with Ethan gone and a baby to be the sole caretaker for. There was something about Zoe that made him think he could handle this. That was both a good and a bad thing. But he was only going to focus on the good, because the bad could also be good if he had the time to do something about it, which he didn't.

Chapter Nine

"You know, going out for brownies and milkshakes is really not the best thing to do after we just spent an hour shaking our butts to lose weight," Jocelyn Reisinger said, then took a bite of said brownie.

Zoe snickered after taking a sip of her milkshake with its load of malt and chocolate. "No one's forcing you, and I didn't see you order one of those fruit cups they had available in the case."

"Psh, I'm not going to sit here eating fruit while you chow down on a brownie. That would be torture." She flung a hand over her brow and fell back against the plush, maroon velvet chair at Jitters.

"And I would hate to torture you after you just tortured me with all the Latin dancing. That just wouldn't be fair."

Jocelyn straightened in her chair. "There is that, but we aren't going to talk about it. Nobody makes you take my classes."

"I know, calm your horses. I'm kidding. I love your classes, even if you did make us do double-time on that last one."

"I like the double-time. It makes me feel less ridiculous for sitting here eating a brownie."

"Whatever makes your boat float."

"All right, enough chit-chat. Tell me about how it's going with Dexter Zegray." She leaned forward in her chair with her elbows on her knees. Her perfectly straight black hair had slid out of its ponytail fifteen minutes ago and looked like she had just walked out of a salon. Zoe knew *she* looked like she had run up a hill towing a car full of kids with a tether in her mouth. No part of her had been able to escape the towel she brought to every class, because she'd been dripping sweat when she and the other fifteen women in the class had been put through the paces by Jocelyn.

And here she was ready to put her through the paces in another way. Zoe was prepared, however, and was not going to give more than the bare minimum of details.

"Things have been working out fine. He drops her off, he picks her up, they go home, and I go to sleep. Nothing to it."

Jocelyn smirked. "How was dinner last night? My cousin, Danica, said he was happy she knew what you liked at Joey's because he was afraid of getting it wrong."

Ah, the joys of small-town living and being friends with someone who was practically related to the whole town in one way or another.

"It was nothing. He had to work later, so he offered to bring dinner, and then I got Phoebe ready for bed, and he left."

"No hanky-panky? No moony eyes over his spaghetti, where you each took an end of a noodle and met in the middle with your lips?"

"Have you been in your niece's movie drawer again? I'm no Lady and I'm beginning to wonder if he is no Tramp." She took another sip of her coffee to choke down anything else she might have said.

"Ah-ha! So there is a softening there. I see it in your eyes! Every other time we've talked about this guy, they've shot fire, but now there're little fairy lights twinkling in them."

Zoe put a hand over her eyes to shield any twinkling. They were not twinkling. She would not let them twinkle, no matter what. The ground rules were set between them, and there was no reason to change them now. Dex had been clear about his intentions, or lack thereof, and she was not going to run across that line and throw herself at him. Especially because there were still all those bouquets she'd made for other women, all hanging out in the forefront of her mind.

"Coming to realize?" Jocelyn dragged Zoe's hand away from her face. "Spill!"

So she told her about him asking if she missed Justin and really listening to her answer. About how caring and strong and amazing he was. She could have gone on, but she stopped herself just in time. She hadn't forgotten those flowers, no matter how smitten she sounded in her own mind.

"Why on earth are you here instead of with him, then? Not that I'd want you to miss class, but he would be more important. He's been chasing you for months, and you've been running like a rabbit with a wolf on your tail, only to find out it's another rabbit—and you're sitting here with me?"

"I like sitting here with you. And I still think he might have a bunch of ladies he sends flowers to, which made him a serial dater before now. A child changed that, yeah, but that doesn't make the change permanent." Zoe set her milkshake glass down and took up her brownie. The better to cram her mouth with in case Jocelyn asked more questions, which she probably would. It was in her nature.

Her friend squinted at her while she tilted her head. "It's the pickle jar thing, isn't it?"

Zoe almost choked on the brownie. With a whole lot of effort she forced herself to swallow around the lump in her throat. "What?"

"You heard me. It's the pickle jar thing. You're not going to get close to him because you're afraid you're going to loosen his pickle jar for someone else to twist that lid right off and marry him. Then you'll be making his wedding flowers and going to celebrate his marriage."

She should not have brought him up at all. She absolutely should not have, and now it was time to pay up.

She opened her mouth to protest, but Jocelyn cut her off.

"Before you deny it, be aware I'm going to know if you're lying." Her green eyes flashed with disapproval.

Zoe sighed. Jocelyn would know and would be merciless about jabbing her until she admitted it. "Okay, look, it is partly the pickle jar thing." She kept right on talking over her friend's crow of victory. "It's also that he believes he can't raise this little girl with the interference of dating anyone."

That shut Jocelyn up, though her mouth hung open. As Claudia often said, the fish impression was not attractive.

How much to tell without revealing the past that Dex didn't want out there for public consumption? "He took on Ethan at a young age and did it all with a very focused determination. He had no help. And other than a babysitter, he doesn't want any this time, either. He's afraid any relationship will take away from the time he should be spending with Phoebe." Although he still didn't touch the baby unless he had to. That, however, was not something she was going to share.

Jocelyn got her wits back about her quickly enough. "That's horse pucky."

A surprised laugh burst out of Zoe. "I haven't heard that in ages."

"I'm trying to work on my swearing. That's not the point, though. The point is that it is always easier with two. How could it not be easier to have someone to talk to when things get tough, who's as invested in the situation as you are?"

"That's what he believes, and I'm not the one to tell him he's wrong."

"But you could be the one to prove him wrong," Jocelyn said before sitting back in her chair and eyeing Zoe as Claudia and May had when they wanted her to take on the babysitting gig.

"Nope, I'm respecting his wishes."

"You're hiding behind his handy excuse."

Zoe slurped on her milkshake. "Call it what you want, but it's still not happening. Now tell me about that date you went on last week."

"I'll let you distract me because it is a funny story, but we will come back to this. I reserve the right to harass you to do something about this."

"So, the date was funny?" Zoe said with a smile. She was not going to let Jocelyn take her to task at another time, but it was enough to give her the illusion. For sanity's sake, she couldn't even think about it anymore because it made her all too aware that she was dangerously close to being the pickle jar loosener against her will.

Later that night, though, Claudia called to check in with her, and it all came pouring out again. This time with the irritation that she hadn't let show earlier with Jocelyn.

"What am I going to do?" she asked Claudia over the phone.

"You're going to get a bottle of wine ready because I'll be there in four minutes. This is a girl thing and you're my girl. Oh, and put out some cheese and crackers; dinner feels like it was hours ago."

She was ready in under three and welcomed Claudia with a hug.

"Hey, little sister, I like what you've done with the place."

Zoe had been going over to Claudia and Nate's house when she saw them because it was easier for one person to maneuver than it was for three. So Claudia hadn't seen the changes Zoe had made over the last few weeks since she'd finally let herself fully realize the apartment was hers to do with as she chose and no one else was going to be here when she came home anymore.

"Thanks, just a few things here and there."

Claudia wandered around touching the new things, and Zoe was forced to admit there were a few more than a few. Though she acknowledged it was ridiculous, she still couldn't help but feel Claudia might be mad that she'd changed the space they'd lived in together for years.

"Do you really like it?" she blurted out.

"Of course I do. It's very you and very cozy. I wish

we would have done a couple of these things when I was still here."

"Huh." She viewed the apartment through Claudia's eyes and admitted that some of this might have appealed to Claudia, but they'd changed little except the level at which the knickknacks were kept as Justin got older. "Well, I love your new place."

"It's home," Claudia said with a small smile.

And that hit Zoe in the gut just a little. Because, despite what she'd done in here, it didn't feel any more like the home Claudia appeared to be thinking about.

"So, where's the wine and cheese, because we have a lot to talk about, and I want to get started."

Once they were outfitted for sitting and discussing, Zoe jumped right in. "You know this is going to kill me, but you might have been right. Dex is pretty close to amazing, if I discount the whole sending-flowers-to-lots-of-women thing."

"Of course I was right. And you should discount that. You know you've dated almost as many men as you've sent flowers to his women. Don't jerk back because he's thoughtful."

"You're killing me, and so is he because, now that I've figured out he's amazing, he's completely off limits."

"I highly doubt he's as off limits as you think he is." She popped a cube of cheddar into her mouth and raised an eyebrow at Zoe.

"No, really. I had the same conversation with Jocelyn earlier, and she didn't believe me, either, but he is completely off limits."

"It's the pickle jar loosener thing, isn't it?"

Zoe groaned. "It is, okay? I might be able to

convince him to take a chance, but then he won't stay, and he'll end up married to someone else, and I'll have to do his engagement flowers and the flowers for the mother of the bride, and you'll do his cake, and May will sew the woman's dress, and it will be a beautiful wedding, and I'll have made it happen, but for once I will be so freaking torn up about it that I won't be able to handle myself." By the end of that one run-on sentence her cheeks felt flushed and her voice had gone up an octave.

"So you'll just have to make him think—know—that there is no one better out there for him than you."

"If only it were that easy."

"It will be, my darling sister. For one thing, we have an inside woman with May, and for two, we haven't gone wrong yet on the matches being pushed, including my own, especially my own. So whip out those flirting games you tried to teach me and make him have eyes for no one but you."

Yeah, well, she never had any problem getting them; it was keeping them that she hadn't yet mastered.

****

"Are you sure May doesn't mind us being here?"

"May is right here, you big lug, and she does not mind at all." The ultimate mother, in Dex's eyes, came in with her daughter strapped to her chest in some sling-like thing. The little girl's eyes were closed, and her little mouth was slack as she slept soundly.

"Should we be quiet?" he whispered, afraid to wake up the baby.

"Heavens, no." May put down a plate of chicken casserole in front of him on the dining room table, then another in front of Brad. "Make all the noise you want.

She's going to have to get used to sleeping through anything when I have her at the shop."

"Hon, I told you I would get the food." Brad rose from his chair, placed a kiss on his wife's neck, and made her sit down as he headed to the kitchen for her plate.

"Always taking care of me." She smiled fondly after Brad before narrowing her eyes at Dex. "So tell me, how's it going with Zoe? And don't pull any punches. She can be prickly, but she also has a heart of pure goodness."

"You don't have to tell me." He put a napkin on his lap and prepared to dig in.

"Before you start, let me say the casserole came from Brad's aunt, so I can't completely vouch for how good it's going to be. I will, however, be able to tell her that we ate it. If it's not good, then I'm sure we have about ten other things to heat up in a flash."

"I'm sure this will be fine." He took a bite and watched as May smoothed her hand over Lucinda's head and crooned to her. She talked with her, too, constantly keeping her hand on her somewhere. In contrast, Phoebe sat in her carrier, holding onto her turtle, sucking her thumb and staring at him as if waiting for something. Damn, he should at least get her out. But then he wouldn't be able to eat, and he'd probably drop her. He had thought about bringing the playpen for her to hang out in, but that had felt like too much work for a few hours. Now he wished he had taken the time to throw it into the back of the car.

"So how are things going?" Brad asked as he came back in bearing a plate for May and a glass of water. He, too, stroked the baby's head as he passed by, placing a kiss on her crown.

Okay, now he felt like an ass. Putting down his fork, he unstrapped Phoebe from her carrier and placed her on his lap facing the table. Of course, the first thing she did was make a grab for his fork. He jerked back, and she almost fell out of his lap. He sucked at this.

"Could be better," he said, placing Phoebe's turtle in her hands and hoping it might distract her while he ate the rest of his dinner.

"Have you heard from Ethan yet?" Brad took a bite off his plate and looked at May. "This isn't half bad. At least we can honestly say this didn't get thrown in the trash this time."

May swatted his arm. "Be nice. She's your aunt. Just be glad there wasn't paprika or jalapeno juice in it this time."

"Maybe she learned her lesson from before." Brad placed his hand over May's on the table, and it was all Dex could do not to think of Zoe's hand and his own.

"So, Ethan?" May turned to Dex again.

"Nothing so far." Even with one hand wrapped tightly around her turtle, Phoebe still made a second grab for the fork. He was going to have to wait to eat. Pushing back his plate, he held Phoebe on his knee with both hands at her waist. He had no idea what to do with her, but this seemed the safest position.

"He's not even answering your texts?" Brad shoveled another forkful in, making Dex hungrier than he had been before. Maybe he could put Phoebe on the floor and eat. Then again, the last time he'd had her on the floor she'd ended up with a huge welt on her head. No, thanks.

"You know, Dex, we have a playpen in the next

room, if you want Brad to drag it in. Then Phoebe can hang out while you eat."

Relief coursed through him. Brad was up from his chair again before he could say anything and took Phoebe out of Dex's hands, nuzzling her stomach and making her laugh before laying her down on her back in the mesh-sided playpen. Her thumb went back into her mouth, and she stared at him, again.

He made quick work of his food and kept the talk to mundane things or sports. He'd asked how Lucinda was earlier and hadn't understood half of what May had said about percentiles and growth charts.

Glancing at the clock, he realized it was only six thirty. What was he going to do with Phoebe for the rest of the night? He couldn't very well stay here until bedtime and take away from Brad and May's time with Lucinda just because he was feeling selfish.

"I should probably take Phoebe home and let you guys get settled in for the night. Thanks for the dinner." He picked up his plate and walked through the doorway to the kitchen. Phoebe sent up a wail like nothing he had ever heard.

Rushing back to the dining room, he was afraid she'd hurt herself again. But nothing looked out of place, and she stopped crying. He still had his plate in his hands, so he walked it to the kitchen again. And again, Phoebe screamed bloody murder.

This time he dropped off the plate and came back to stand over the playpen. She sniffled, but just stared at him as he stared back at her.

"Does she cry when you leave her with Zoe?" May asked, standing next to him.

"No, never. She barely looks at me when she's

with Zoe. She's never cried when I left her."

"But have you ever left her with anyone but Zoe?" Brad said from his other side.

"Well, no."

"And you're with her when Zoe's not?" Brad leaned down and picked up Phoebe. She nestled right into him but kept her eyes on Dex, like she was afraid if she looked away he'd leave again.

"Always."

Brad smoothed a hand down Phoebe's back and she curled tighter into him, her thumb in her mouth, the turtle clutched tight. "I wonder if she's suffering from abandonment. Do you think she knows her mom left her?"

They all stared at Phoebe. Did she have abandonment issues? Did she realize her mom had left her, her father had run away, and all she had left was an inept uncle who would do right by her but couldn't promise anything more than a roof and three squares?

It was more than some kids had, but he couldn't help feeling that he was going to be striving her whole life for something he'd never achieve.

Chapter Ten

"Isn't she the cutest thing?" Mona cooed at Phoebe on Thursday morning. Dex had dropped her off about twenty minutes ago, and Mona had scooped her right up. "Look at this face!" Mona tickled her chin, making Phoebe squeal.

"She's adorable," Zoe said, her mind on the flower arrangement request that had just come in. "Do you have her for a few minutes while I get this together?"

"No problem." Mona took the baby around the shop, leaving Zoe to do her thing.

An hour later, she looked up to find Mona dancing across the floor with Phoebe, a look of pure adoration on her face. She sang the lyrics of the instrumental song playing over the speakers. There weren't any customers in the shop, but that wouldn't have stopped her anyway.

Zoe took a moment to relax against the counter and just enjoy the show. It had been a long time since Mona had had a baby around, and she was wonderful with them. She had always been very involved with Justin even while she had hoped for an easier path for Claudia.

"You look good with her," Zoe said.

"I love babies. You know that." Mona's smile beamed from her face. "Now I just need my daughters to provide me with more. May did her job; when are you going to do yours?"

Claudia chose that moment to come out of the back kitchen. "Yeah, Zoe, when are you going to do your baby-making job?" she said, laughter evident in her voice.

"I might want to find a guy who sticks around first."

"That would help. Fortunately, you have one right under your nose, if you'd look."

Zoe blew out a breath. "I've already explained that it's not going to happen with Dex. I don't know why you keep harping on it." No longer amused, Zoe turned back to the floral arrangement.

"And I don't know why you won't go for it." Claudia came over to stand next to Zoe and nudge her with an elbow.

"Are we having this conversation again?"

"I haven't had it yet," Mona chimed in. "So yes, let's have it again."

"Zoe doesn't want to go after Dex, even though she's wondering if maybe her impression of him was wrong from the beginning. For one, he said he's not going to have time for dating, with the baby."

"Rubbish!" Mona kissed Phoebe on the forehead. "Things are always easier with two. He's smart enough to know that."

Zoe rolled her eyes. "He might be smart enough, but he's convinced that since he devoted all his time to raising Ethan from the time he was twelve that he has to do the same thing with Phoebe."

"He raised his brother?"

She was treading on territory she wasn't supposed to share. "It's not my story, Mom. Suffice it to say that Dex feels his plate is full enough. Ethan isn't returning his phone calls, he's depending on me to watch Phoebe during the day so he can work, and he has his hands full with her at night."

"But the two of you together would make a great team, and it would spread out the handful at night." In Mona's world, that was the way you did things. Zoe understood it, but she wasn't going to take the time to make Dex see that only to have him realize someone else would be even better at helping him.

"And then we have the pickle jar thing." Claudia took Phoebe from a protesting Mona and snuggled her.

"I'm not having that conversation again." How was it that Claudia could almost read her mind?

"That one is long overdue." Mona took the baby back, making Phoebe laugh and pat her head. "You just have chosen the wrong men, my dear. It has nothing to do with you."

Apparently they were having this conversation after all. "Look, once or twice dating a guy who marries the girl right after me…" Zoe shrugged. "It happens. But I'm at twelve, last count. And the common denominator there is me. You have to admit it."

"I will do no such thing." Mona put her free arm around Zoe, and Phoebe patted her face. "It was just the men you chose. Looking back at it, is there a single one from your past that you could see yourself with, long term? Or did you dodge twelve bullets by not settling for someone who didn't get all of you?"

She'd never thought of it that way, and she didn't have time to do so now, because the Stevenson wedding party had just walked in for all three kinds of services that Decadence offered. But she tucked it away for later, because maybe her mom had a point. Not that she'd admit it out loud since Mona's head would swell, but it definitely was worth tossing around in the quiet of her apartment tonight.

****

Saturday was finally here. Dex rested against the headboard and listened through the monitor to Phoebe snoozing away in her crib. She'd been up three times last night for a bottle, but now she was sleeping. He'd like to be sleeping, too, but his brain was awake and clicking away.

The first week with Zoe as babysitter extraordinaire was down, and so far so good. If he thought about her too much at odd times during the day, then that was his own fault. Not for the first time he wished they could have been together before Phoebe came into their lives. At least if the beginnings of a relationship had been in process, he would have known whether or not it was worth spreading himself thin enough to do it all.

That was not relevant anymore. What he did have to think about was the fact that he had Phoebe all weekend to himself and no real plans for what to do with her. They could play on her blanket, and he could read her a story, but that was about twenty minutes out of the next forty-eight hours.

Massaging his head, he picked up the book he'd purchased at the baby store. It listed the many things Phoebe should be doing. He hadn't had time to read it before, but he took the time now. Who knew when he'd have a quiet moment again?

He started making a list of all the things she should be doing and eating. That at least would fill up another hour, or so, since he had to head to the grocery store for baby cereal and probably a teething device. He could do it the way his parents did, with a finger full of whiskey, but that might not be ideal.

Halfway through the book, Dex realized Phoebe still hadn't made a sound. It would be a record if she was still asleep, and he should enjoy it, but he couldn't fight the feeling that something was wrong.

Jumping out of bed, he threw on a T-shirt and hustled down the hall to her room. Only to find her curled around her turtle, still sleeping the sleep of the innocent.

And she really was an innocent. She'd had no part in how she'd gotten here. It wasn't her fault both her parents were boneheads. She was so sunny and happy despite the trauma of her short life so far, and that was more valuable than anything.

He lightly drew a path down her cheek with his index finger. She was so soft, so fragile. Until she gripped his finger and nearly yanked him off balance because he wasn't ready for the move. She tucked his hand under her head with the turtle, her eyes still closed.

A smile pulled at his lips. She might be little, but she was also fierce, and that fierceness was something that would get her through. He used the back of his other hand to brush her hair back off her face. She opened her eyes and immediately smiled at him.

How could that expression not melt your heart?

Picking her up out of the crib, he cuddled her close and kissed the top of her head. She turned her face up and gave him a sloppy kiss on the cheek with her mouth wide open.

Laughing and drool had never felt so good. He'd

offer her far more than three squares and a roof. He was in love with this little girl and would do anything for her. Whether Ethan ever came back or not, Phoebe would know she was loved. Dex wouldn't have it any other way.

His cell rang in his bedroom, but he ignored it to settle into a rocking chair in the corner of Phoebe's room. He rocked her and hummed to her as she played with his fingers, his stubbly beard, and her toes.

She was not a burden and would never think she was. He could do nothing less than make sure of that.

The doorbell rang next. That he couldn't ignore. With Phoebe securely in his arms, he made his way downstairs, running a hand though his hair and hoping it wasn't sticking straight up from his head. It didn't matter. If someone ventured near his door this early on a Saturday morning, then they could just deal with bedhead.

He regretted that decision immediately when he saw Zoe standing on his doorstep. But she saw him through the sidelights on the door, so he couldn't exactly run away without answering.

"Hey," she said when he opened the door.

He didn't throw it all the way open, but she was going to see him, anyway. "Hey. What has you up and out so early?"

"Flower delivery for a wedding at ten a.m. means getting up at five to make sure everything is in order." She looked delicious standing at his door in tight jeans, a form-fitting pink shirt, and old sneakers.

He cleared his throat. "And was everything in order?"

"Of course." Her smile was brilliant.

"Well, that's great." He wasn't sure what else to say. She had seen him in his pajamas sans shirt before, when she'd had to wake them up, but he hadn't planned that, and having her in his house now felt too intimate, too contradictory to what he'd told himself he wanted, to raise Phoebe without the mess of anything more on his plate.

"I came by to see if you wanted to do something with Phoebe today. Even though it's your day off, I thought maybe you'd still like some help. I don't have anything pressing to get back to at the shop until one."

"Uh, that would be great."

"I can come back after you're dressed." The smile turned sly, and he laughed.

"Come on in now. If you want to get Phoebe ready, I can do the same for myself, and then maybe we could go to breakfast."

"Sounds good. I'm starving."

"Me, too." He tried not to look at her when he said those words, since seeing her on his doorstep made him hungrier for far more than pancakes or eggs.

****

Step one accomplished, and she had managed to not even drool over him and his sticking-up hair. The man had both amazing and adorable wrapped tightly into one package that made her insides feel like they were on fire. This was either her best idea or her worst.

After going home on Thursday she had thought long and hard about what Mona and Claudia said, about what May had said too, and had come to the conclusion that even if she was the pickle jar loosener, at some point it would have to be her turn.

And so here she was, after negotiating time off

with Claudia and delivering the wedding flowers extra early so she could be done until one. Her hands felt sweaty and her brain a little bit on the fritz because she'd never pursued anyone before. She tried to remember the things she'd told Claudia to do when she was going after Nate, but none of them applied to her and her unique situation. How did you go about convincing someone who did not want a relationship that you were worth the risk?

She was about to find out.

Setting Phoebe on the diaper-changing table, Zoe kept a hand on her belly as she reached for a new diaper. After changing her and giving her a little raspberry on her tummy, they went to the closet, where Zoe picked out a cute little number with ruffles on the sleeves.

"We're going to have fun this morning, Phoebster. Are you ready for some fun?"

"Phoebster?" Dex said from the doorway with a chuckle. Zoe turned to find him leaning against the doorjamb with his ankles crossed, his arms crossed, and a smile on his handsome face that made her heart flip in her chest.

"Yep, Phoebster." She finished snapping the outfit together over the diaper and lifted her up to nuzzle her belly. Phoebe grabbed Zoe's hair and shrieked, making Zoe and Dex laugh.

"Are you sure you want to take her to a restaurant? We might be better off picking up some bagels and going to a park."

"The park is after breakfast. I'm sure she'll be fine." She smoothed down her hair, wondering if she looked like Dex had this morning with his bedhead.

"We'd better take the stroller then."

"Look at you, getting the hang of this packing-for-baby stuff."

"It's all logic, my dear." He tipped an imaginary hat. "I'll meet you downstairs."

Such a generic endearment shouldn't have done things to her insides, but she was coming to realize that everything about Dex was worth a tingle or two.

She met him at the car, and they got underway.

"Anywhere in particular you want to go?" he asked at the stop sign at the top of his street.

"Wherever you like. I'm not picky as long as they have creamed chipped beef."

"A woman after my own heart," he said, turning to give her a smile.

He had no idea.

****

"So then he comes back for 'I'm sorry' flowers for the third time, and I told him he might want to just write me a check for my vacation fund, and I'll send flowers every other day."

Dex hadn't laughed this much in a long while. It felt good, to say the least.

"And did he write you that check?" He put another dab of the creamed chipped beef sauce on the baby spoon and let Phoebe taste it. She grabbed his hand and shoved the spoon in her mouth.

"He just left me his credit card number and told me to keep the deliveries coming for the next month. Every other day like clockwork. His wife and I got to be friends. When I delivered the flowers we'd have coffee. Then she left him and moved to Arizona. We still talk. She finally found someone who only has to send her flowers because he loves her, not because he's a jerk."

Dragging the spoon through the sauce on his plate again, he took in the woman across the table from him. She was vibrant, beautiful, and so full of fun. Being with her was like playing hooky no matter where they were.

He gave the spoon to Phoebe this time, who stuck it in her mouth, then pulled it out and proceeded to bang it on the tray. Fortunately the tray was plastic, so it didn't make that much noise.

"What park are we going to?" He sat back in his chair to avoid the temptation of taking Zoe's hand in his own.

"I was thinking the one over on Lincoln. You and I could play some miniature golf. I bet Phoebe will get a kick out of seeing the windmills and the bridges from her stroller."

"That works for me. I hope you brought your A game, though, because I play a mean round of mini-golf."

He'd lost her. Somewhere in the middle of his mock challenge, something had pulled her attention away.

He started to turn in his chair, but she grabbed his hand.

"Please don't look. I'm trying to avoid eye contact, or they'll come over," she said in what was almost a whisper.

"Who are we avoiding?" he whispered back.

"No one now," she answered quietly through a fake smile and clenched teeth. "Kevin, hi! How are you?"

Kevin leaned over, and he and Zoe did an awkward one-armed-hug thing while Zoe continued to wear that fake smile.

"Hey, Zo! I'm so glad I saw you! How's it going? Is this your family? I'm glad you found someone finally."

"Uh, things are good."

What should he do? They weren't a family. But if she wanted to avoid this guy, and from what he'd just said, there must be some history here, he couldn't break that for her.

"I want you to meet Winnie. Things with Petrina didn't work out, but now I found Winnie, and I know what I was missing."

Winnie looked remarkably like a dulled-down version of Zoe, in Dex's opinion. He was pretty schooled in body language, and he was getting the vibe that Zoe was supremely uncomfortable.

"I'm glad things are going well for you, Kevin." She gestured in Dex's direction. "This is Dex and Phoebe." She moved right along. "It's nice to meet you, Winnie. Are you from the area?"

"I will be now." She flashed out her left hand. "Kevin just asked me to marry him."

"Which is why I was looking for you, Zoe." He turned a charming smile on her, or at least that was what Dex assumed he was going for. It wasn't working, regardless.

"Me?" Zoe's cheeks must have been hurting from that false grin. She looked like she might crack, but he didn't know how to help her.

"Yeah, I was wondering if you would be willing to do the flowers for the wedding."

Winnie jumped in. "We were at Cooper and Melanie's wedding two weeks ago, and the arrangements were just beautiful. I don't want anyone but you to do the flowers, because you're the best," she gushed. "And Kevin's mom said there is nowhere else except Decadence to get the best cakes and dress."

"Of course she did," Zoe said with a flat tone to her voice that obviously Kevin and the future Mrs. Kevin did not catch.

"Does this mean you'll do it?" Winnie squealed, clapping her hands like a toddler.

Phoebe also clapped her hands together, mimicking the woman. A real smile peeked out on Zoe's face. They would definitely be talking about this after they got these two to move on.

"Call Claudia and let her know to set up a time. We'll figure it out. When is the big day?"

"Six months. Is that enough time?" Winnie clasped her hands in front of her chest.

"Zoe will make it happen, won't you, Zoe?" Kevin said.

The fake smile was back. "Of course. I'll see you in a few weeks to get started."

"Thank you!" Winnie came in for a hug that Zoe grimaced through. Kevin tried, too, but Zoe went with the one-armed thing again. Somehow Dex was sure this story was going to be a good one.

Chapter Eleven

"How about that park?" Zoe laid her napkin on the table. Her appetite had fled when Kevin approached. She was ready to get out of here and away from everything. She'd really just like to go back to the shop and book every appointment they had for the next century, but she'd promised Dex she'd hang around until one. She was not going to go back on that promise.

"How about you tell me what that was all about?" Dex leaned back against the booth with his arms crossed while Phoebe blinked at her like an owl with the spoon in her mouth.

"It was about nothing." She linked her fingers together on the table in front of her. "I'm ready to bring my A game to mini-golf." She smiled but had a feeling it fell short when Dex continued to stare at her as if he wasn't moving until she spilled.

She sighed. The sooner she got this over with, the sooner she could escape. "That was my first boyfriend, this is his second marriage. He wants me to make the flowers. I will. End of story."

"No, there's more here than that. I believe that's part of it, but not all."

This was not a fun pickle jar loosener story, and she was not going to tell him the truth. Seeing Kevin didn't hurt as much as she had thought it would, but it still brought an ache to the scars he'd left.

"Look, he's the only boyfriend I've ever had who I haven't done the flowers and the whole wedding for. I thought I was done, but I guess I have one more and *then* I'm done."

"And how many does this make?"

She tried to mumble, but he still caught what she said.

"Twelve? You've done the weddings for twelve guys?"

"I have."

"You've dated twelve guys?"

"That's not so many. A lot of them weren't very serious, and they got married to the very next woman they dated, so the time frame wasn't that big."

"A lot of them married the next girl, or every one of them married the woman right after you?"

Mumbling hadn't worked last time, so this time she owned it. "Every single one married the very next girl. Every single one." She clenched her hands until her knuckles turned white. "Can we go to the park now? I feel the need to take a whack at some balls."

And then his hand was over her clenched fingers, and he pried her fingers open to hold her left hand. "They had no idea what they missed out on. They were all idiots."

She put her free hand over her eyes. "Thanks. It doesn't change the fact that now I have to fit one more wedding in there. But I don't have any more ex-boyfriends to pass along to other girls, so we should be good to go." She moved her hand out from under his. "I'll get the check if you can get Phoebe."

"Let's do that the other way around and we're

golden. Then we'll let you whack some balls."

Ten minutes later she was doing just that and having a great time. Dex really was a good miniature golfer, and she had no trouble keeping up with him. They were neck and neck with scores, and Phoebe had squealed her way through the whole medieval-themed course.

"Second to the last hole," Dex said, setting up his ball. They'd flipped a coin and he had won the option of going first. She was glad he had, because it allowed her to not only watch his moves but also emulate his game. She was three points over his score. If she could get him to mess up this one and then not get a good score on the last hole, she could potentially win. Although at this point, she was just happy for the distraction from Kevin and his new fiancée. She wouldn't care if she were going to lose soundly to Dex.

That didn't mean she was going to go down without a fight now, though. She was too close to winning to let him have it without a challenge.

It wasn't her fault if she accidentally brushed up against him while he took his first swing. She'd wanted to touch him for days, and this was as good an excuse as any. Especially because the prize was twofold. Didn't he have just the firmest rear end she'd ever have the pleasure of brushing up against? He looked so solid, but to feel it was a different matter.

He went for a second whack at the little green ball, and she made sure to lean over Phoebe's stroller facing him. The shirt she'd worn wasn't indecent, but if you leaned just right, you could give a glimpse of a little more than you anticipated—unless you anticipated enticing. And she had and it did. His eyes bulged a little

111

as his golf club wobbled over his shoulder.

"Is it my turn yet?" she asked, all innocence.

"It might as well be." He groaned. "You know, if we were playing pool I'd call this hustling, but I'm not sure there's a name for it when you're in the midst of eighteen small castles."

"Unfair?" She laughed. It felt so good. As good as it felt to be with Dex. Maybe her mom was right. Maybe she'd just been dating the wrong guys. And maybe Dex was wrong in his thinking, too, and they could make this work with the baby. There didn't have to be drama when dating, they could make it smooth between the two of them. They were both adults, intelligent adults.

"How hard and fast is your rule about not dating because you're raising Phoebe?"

He stood for a moment and really looked at her. She felt the look like it was a caress, and it did things she might be afraid of becoming addicted to but also wanted more than she was afraid.

"It worked last time." He set the club down and leaned on it. "I don't know if I have the time to spend with anyone like I would if I were dating them. I also don't want people coming in and out of Phoebe's life. It's one of the reasons I stayed single when I was raising Ethan. Less confusion that way. Phoebe's already been abandoned. I don't know if I can do that again to her if someone decided we're not right for them."

"And what if you were to decide the woman wasn't right for you?" She stood behind Phoebe's stroller, gripping the handle. This was all hypothetical and really a ridiculous conversation since he had already said no. And despite her earlier desire to date him, she couldn't deny his track record wasn't exactly stellar.

"Again there would be someone else in Phoebe's life who had gone away. It's better if I don't start anything I have no intention of finishing."

"Why wouldn't you finish?"

"I phrased that wrong. I don't want to start anything I can't put my whole attention on."

"So you're really going to stay celibate for eighteen years?"

His face blanched. "I don't know what the future holds, but for right now, yes. Could you imagine me bringing someone into this mess at this point? I'm waiting for Ethan to come home, and juggling my job, and essentially being a single dad." He ran a hand over his hair. "Until Ethan returns, my life has to revolve around Phoebe. I can't think about anything else."

Well, that answered that question. Besides, she had enough on her plate, too. Starting a relationship with someone she didn't completely trust would be ridiculous. Then again, the more she was near him, the more she wanted him. She'd come to the conclusion she might have let his thoughtfulness to other women blind her to the fact that it really was kind to send flowers after a date. But did she want to actually pursue someone who was adamant he did not want a relationship?

Then again, it could break her pickle jar streak if she dated someone with absolutely no intentions. It was all making her head swim.

He'd already said he wasn't interested in anyone now that he had Phoebe to take care of. Was she actually going to want him to want her after she'd spent months avoiding him? Especially now when he was unavailable? Surely she wasn't that perverse.

She looked over at him, taking in his masculine profile and the way he stood casually leaning on the club.

Yep, she was that perverse.

****

The light spicy scent Zoe used had been driving Dex crazy all day. He lined up his shot for the last hole and inhaled, then exhaled. She got caught in his nose, again. He might never get it out of his senses. And yet he found he didn't want to. All that talk about dating made him wonder if she was hinting at more for them. But she'd never let him near her when he was free, so why would she want him now that he wasn't?

Squaring his shoulders, he hit the little ball and waited for it to go into one of the three holes. He'd never won a free game here, but there might be a first time for everything. Including Zoe acting as if she might be interested in him.

He turned to look at her after the ball went in the "three" hole to find her crowing like a damn bird. He had not been on top of his game today. How could he be, when she stood across from him in that tight shirt? His mind might have been made up about no dating, but that didn't mean he wasn't fully aware she was a woman—a woman he had lusted over for months before this whole Phoebe kerfuffle had come up.

"Your shot."

"I'm only one point away from you, so if I get a two, we're tied. If I get a one, you lose."

"I highly doubt I'm going to lose."

"We'll see about that, buster." She leaned over to

put her ball on the ground, and he couldn't help but notice the way her curves strained the seams of her jeans. She was put together in a way that had made him stand up and pay attention the very first time they met. In Al's office she had been jaw dropping, even in her old, ratty clothes. And he'd thought they'd made a connection—until he'd introduced himself, and she'd gone cold like a block of ice.

He'd debated asking what had happened that afternoon, considered it ever since she'd signed on as babysitter, but he was afraid to upset the apple cart for information he could do nothing with.

Maybe, after their previous conversation, now was a good time to ask.

"So what about you? I heard the many now-married boyfriends story, but are you dating anyone at the moment? Anyone who would be jealous that you're out playing miniature golf with me?"

She straightened, nudged the ball with the toe of her sneaker, and shot him a smile. "Nope, no one at the moment. I don't have anyone to send flowers to, either."

"You know, that's the second reference you've made to my flowers in conjunction with dating. I'm not sure why. Is that a problem for you? I thought you'd be happy to have the business. Your uncle was the one to suggest you."

"It's great. No worries." And there was that fake smile, again.

A light bulb came on in his head that had previously not been there. Did she think he'd dated all the women he sent flowers to? Holy shit, that would make his social calendar filled with a different date almost every night to keep up with all of them. But it would explain her hostility after she heard his name, and the way she'd fended him off for months while he continued to send flowers to other women.

She missed the shot, also going into the three and stamping her feet while muttering under her breath. To make matters worse, Phoebe clapped from her stroller. Dex had an idea of how to show her how wrong she was without him having to say a word.

Chapter Twelve

After a snack at one of the food kiosks in the park, Dex loaded Phoebe into the car without Zoe's help. He was getting the hang of taking care of this little girl. She'd also noticed that he touched her more often and talked to her in a way he hadn't before. Hopefully that meant he was coming to terms with his situation, instead of the resentment and the cold duty he'd first exhibited.

And now she could go back to the shop to spend the rest of the day thinking about the fact that she wanted him but it would be a long, long time before he'd ever seriously look at her like he had before. She wasn't jealous of Phoebe and certainly didn't blame her for the situation they all found themselves in, but it was damned inconvenient that Zoe had come to realize she might have been unfair to him only after the point was moot.

In her musings, she'd lost track of their direction on the way back to the shop. So to say she was surprised when they pulled into the parking lot of a retirement village was a bit of an understatement. They wound through streets like Relaxation Way and Memory Lane, passing quaint houses and perfectly manicured lawns. Maybe he had another quick errand while they were out this way. She had an hour until she was due back at the shop and was more than happy to

117

spend just a little more time with him. Which was pathetic, but there you had it.

As a lawyer he probably handled many people's wills. Perhaps he had some paperwork he hadn't been able to drop off when this had all happened. Whatever it was, she was going to stay right here.

"Hey, can you come in with me for just a second? I think Phoebe might be ready for a bottle. There's a microwave you can use, inside."

Something made her hesitate, until Phoebe started crying that pitiful whimper that meant she was hungry. "Just for a minute, but then I really need to get back."

His smile held more than just mirth, making her uneasy. She followed him anyway, into the foyer of the large building at the center of the retirement village. Chairs were clustered in conversational circles. Potted plants lined the windows, and soft music played as a backdrop to the peaceful and serene setting.

Dex walked past the reception desk with a smile and a wave to "Nancy," then kept going down an open hallway. Zoe had Phoebe on her hip and the bottle ready to go in the microwave. She trailed along behind Dex, who had a proper diaper bag on his shoulder. No more grocery bags for this little girl's belongings.

Tasteful pictures of seaside cottages and flowers lined the soft yellow walls. Little groupings of chairs and sofas were scattered throughout the place, inviting someone to come and sit, spend some time by the big brick fireplace on the far wall. It didn't smell like antiseptic or a hospital, as the place where her grandmother had lived for five years smelled. It was actually pleasant.

She wondered if they ever needed fresh flowers in

the rooms or community areas and cursed herself for not bringing business cards with her. But then again, it wasn't like she had known they were doing anything more than hanging with Phoebe for the morning.

In almost no time at all they reached a set of double doors framed by tasteful, yet fake, ivy. The words Dining Room were stenciled above the door in big letters with curlicues on the ends. And she was paying such attention to the details so she wouldn't have to acknowledge the hand Dex held out to walk her into the dining room. No, she'd walk alone, thanks very much.

He leaned over, grasped her hand, then gently pushed the door open with a flourish. He stepped back to let her go through first, then took her elbow and led her forward. She spent a brief second considering yanking her arm out from his grasp, but when she saw how many people there were in the room, she decided she didn't want to embarrass herself by making a scene.

Quite a few of the diners were hollering "Hello, Dex!" in voices that sounded quite hearty for people looking so old. A few women waved to him, their silver hair shining in the muted light of the overhead chandeliers.

All she wanted to do was find the microwave so she could heat up the bottle and get on their way. Flower arranging was calling her.

Finally, they arrived at a table filled with women ranging from about age sixty all the way up to what she guessed must be ninety.

"Ladies," Dex said in his wonderful voice that worked its way right into Zoe's bloodstream. He held her elbow more firmly and brought her up to the very edge of the table. "I'd like you all to meet Zoe Bradley from Decadence and tell her that I'm not cheating on her with any one of you—or all of you, for that matter."

She felt her face heat up before any of the women sitting at the table uttered a word. And then her mind started to whirl. She caught less than half of what was being said as they all started chattering about the beautiful bouquets Dex sent them. How they made their days, since all of them had lost their husbands. What a catch Dex was, and how many good things they had all heard about her.

The blush only got worse at the heaped praise about the way she so skillfully put together flowers. How they had all decided to start using her for their florist needs. One woman inquired about what else the shop did. Apparently, she'd seen the business card attached to the flowers, and her granddaughter was getting married sometime soon.

Zoe forced herself to participate in the conversation and answer questions. All the while, she was dying inside. How could she have misjudged so badly? Why did he still even try with her when she'd acted like a queen to a peon when he really was a great guy?

When the ladies got sidetracked talking amongst themselves for a moment about a cribbage game coming up, and wouldn't it be fun to have a special cake made by Claudia, Zoe took her chance, plopped Phoebe into Dex's arms, and excused herself, saying she needed to use the ladies' room. Of course, she had no intention of wandering around trying to find it, but instead walked right out the front doors as soon as she escaped the dining room and all the lovely ladies. She could always plead a case of the cramps if they thought she had been rude in not really saying goodbye. But she had to get the hell out of here and plan for a way to face Dex the next day, even though she'd rather not. She'd promised she'd watch Phoebe and she would stick with that, but at the moment she was way too embarrassed to face him after all the horrible things she'd said and thought about him.

****

She was taking too long. Dex glanced at his watch for the fifth time in two minutes, wondering if Zoe had gotten lost on her way to the bathroom. This was a big place, and it could have happened, he supposed. Phoebe squirmed in his other arm.

"Ladies, I should go check on Zoe, to see if she found the restroom." He rose from the red brocade cushioned chair and shook all the women's hands. He let them kiss the baby, too, as they cooed over her and made him promise to bring her back another day. "If any of you need anything, be sure to give me a call. You know I'm available for you."

When he got to Cheryl Gifford, he gave her hand an extra squeeze. She had been the one to most recently lose her beloved husband. He'd be adding her to his list of women he sent flowers to on a monthly basis, just like Sissy and Thelma and Letitia. His aunt, who had cared for him on and off throughout his teen years, had lost his uncle when Dex was fourteen. He'd never forgotten how devastated she was, or how happy when he'd picked her a clutch of flowers one day on his way home from school. If he remembered correctly, most of them were just pretty weeds, but she'd held them to her chest as if they were a hundred roses. He'd been taken back by his parents shortly after, and hadn't returned until he left for college.

121

Cheryl returned the squeeze, but then held on longer and pulled him down close to her face. "I don't think your Zoe went to the bathroom, since I just saw her running across the lawn in front of the dining room windows. I think you better go after her outside." She let go of his hand and sat back in her chair. "Then again, that's just an old woman's opinion. Unless she frequently pees outside?"

He laughed as she'd meant him to, but inside his stomach was roiling. Maybe his plan to shock her into realizing he wasn't a philanderer had backfired on him and he'd be left alone anyway. He couldn't let that happen.

He sketched a wave at the rest of the table, promising to come see them sometime during the coming week to have tea. And then he booked the hell out of the room like the devil was hot on his heels.

He found her a half mile down the road as he drove slowly with Phoebe strapped in the backseat. Thank God this was a relatively quiet street, because he rolled down the window and tried to talk to her as she walked. No other cars came up behind him, forcing him to speed up.

"Zoe, we need to talk." He leaned over the seat, keeping one eye on the road and glancing at her crossed arms and long stride.

She ignored him, lengthening that stride.

"Please, I want to talk to you." He corrected his steering and veered back away from the curb when he realized he'd almost jumped it while looking at her profile.

Still ignoring him, she sped up. At this rate she'd be able to walk all the way home before he got a chance to talk to her. "Can you please just get in the car? I'll take you right home. I promise not to even talk to you on the way there, if that's what you want."

That got her attention. She halted her steps and glared at him. "Nothing to talk about."

He let that rest for a moment as he waited for her to get in. He left the car idling, got out, and came around to open her door.

She eyed him through squinted lids. "You promise not to talk to me the whole way there?"

God, it would kill him, but maybe he could get her to warm up to him when they arrived at her house. He had a lot riding on this. If she refused to watch Phoebe, he'd be back to square one. "Promise." He crossed his heart and held out a pinky.

The gesture seemed to surprise her. But she unbent long enough to hook her pinky finger through his and say, "Pinky swear."

Then she got into the car and the soft sultry scent of her seemed to permeate the air. He drew in a breath, enjoying the feel of her perfume lingering in his lungs.

She must have taken the movement wrong because she said, "Don't even open your mouth. I was serious about there being no talking."

He exhaled through his nose, figuring he had a long ride in front of him. So of course, this time, they hit every single red light. Phoebe slept in the back, her soft snuffles the only sound in the car. He opened his mouth a few times, but Zoe would say, "Ah, ah, ah," every single time.

Until they got to the last stoplight before her house. And then it was if a flood gate opened. "You know, you could have told me before that you were a philanthropist instead of a philanderer." She hugged herself close and seemed to shrink in the seat next to him. "I felt like an idiot in there, knowing the things I'd said to you and the way I have felt, only to find out you were just being a good guy all this time, and I had no idea. Do you know what that makes me want to do to you?"

He stayed silent because there was no right answer to that question.

She seemed to expect his silence and barreled on. "I've been a bitch, and you didn't even let me know. How stupid you must have thought I was." He'd parked behind her shop by now. She got out before he could help her, and started walking again. It was time to finally say something.

"I never thought you were stupid."

She turned to him, disbelief stamped on her face. "What else could you have possibly thought when I kept saying you were a playboy?"

He grinned sheepishly as he ran a hand over the back of his head. "I guess I thought Brad had told you about my younger days when I couldn't beat the ladies off with a stick. Maybe that you were trying too hard to resist me, finding ways to not be with me, so you decided to make me out to be a bad guy."

She laughed, and the sound ran straight through his stomach, radiating out to other parts of his anatomy that stood quickly to attention. "Have you ever read a romance novel?"

This time he laughed and felt his neck heat up. "Actually my college roommate's girlfriend used to read them all the time. Once when I was sick with the flu and she hung out with me, she tortured me by reading a particularly steamy one that nearly made my ears bleed." It wasn't necessary to tell her that every once in a while he still picked one up at the grocery store and read it before giving it to his friend's now-wife as a gift.

"Truce?" He held out his hand and hoped she'd take it.

"I'll do you one better," she said, grabbing his hand and pulling him in for a kiss that nearly melted the soles off his shoes.

He growled in the back of his throat and took control, kissing her for all he was worth.

"Take me home," she murmured against his lips. "Your home."

He was oh, so very tempted. In fact, he nearly had the car back in drive to make that journey when Phoebe squeaked in the back seat.

His world came crashing back in around his ears. Gentle extraction from her embrace would have been good, but instead he thrust her away. "I can't do this. I'm sorry. I wanted to for months, but I have responsibilities now that come before my own needs." He took in her shocked face and the way she wrapped her arms around her stomach. "Let me walk you up."

****

Zoe walked slowly up the stairs after leaving Dex at his car. She'd refused his offer to walk her up, but he hadn't left yet. That made him a gentleman to wait until she got in the door; however, it made her a fool for continuing to hope he might follow her despite her refusal. After all, turnabout was fair play. She'd kissed him and he'd turned her down. After months of fighting him and her attraction for him because he was a womanizer, today had turned her whole world around. And now he said he had responsibilities that made it impossible for them to be more than nanny and struggling uncle. How could fate be this stupid?

He didn't score on the full scale of gentleman when he didn't wait for her to get to the door. The sound of his car pulling away reached her ears before she was halfway up the outside stairs to her home. She didn't blame him. If he was in as much emotional turmoil as she was right now, then he had every reason.

Letting herself into the apartment, there was still a part of her that expected to see Claudia in the kitchen throwing something together for dinner and Justin tromping down the hallway on feet that were too big for his eleven-year-old body. There'd be a kind of controlled chaos as they shared their days and talked about what to do that night after Justin's homework was done.

Instead, she walked into a space that was dormant, a space that didn't resonate with any sound unless she made it. It was hard being the one left behind even as she was so happy for Claudia.

She ran downstairs to get away from the silence and to finish the rest of an order. But once she was done, she had nowhere else to go but back upstairs.

After putting her purse on the counter, she pulled out a freezer dinner and changed into comfy clothes as she waited for it to be done. To combat the lack of noise, she cranked up her favorite radio station, then pretended Claudia and Justin would be out any minute to have a karaoke showdown to see who knew the most words of any given song on the radio.

But that just depressed her. When the microwave

beeped, she took her food into the living room, lowered the music, and took up the book she'd been meaning to read over the last few weeks. It didn't hold her attention, but at least it was something. Something she had thought she had wanted to do, all the time Claudia and Justin were filling the space and she was wondering what it would be like to actually live on her own. Now that she had it—it sucked.

Also, she hadn't told Dex she would still watch Phoebe, after the silence in the car and the way she had run. She hoped he would assume she wouldn't back out over something as trivial as getting her lust handed back to her, but she didn't know him well enough to be sure. Hell, she hardly knew him at all, and that was more apparent than ever after this afternoon.

In the end, she decided to just text him that she would expect Phoebe Monday morning. He texted her back with the simple words "Thank you" and managed to put yet one more crack in her rearview mirror of him.

She spent Sunday with ice cream, brownies, and sappy love movies on TV that did nothing but make her feel like she had made a huge mistake in not taking Dex up on his offer the very first time she'd met him.

Chapter Thirteen

To say Monday morning was awkward would have been an understatement. Dex wasn't sure if he'd breathe easy again until he was back in the car and on his way to work. First, though, he had to hand off Phoebe and give Zoe her check for the previous week.

How much had she told the other women in her circle? Brad had told him some time ago about emergency girl meetings. Had he been the subject of one? Was Zoe pissed enough by the shoddy way he'd handled things that she'd pulled her feminine wall of protection around her to ward him off?

There was only one way to find out. He really did not want to walk into Decadence and find out he was on anyone's shit list.

Unsnapping the seatbelt from around Phoebe's car seat, Dex caught her looking at him with a grin on her face. "You think this is funny?"

She chortled, waving her turtle around above her head.

"Yeah, it's not funny. I could get my a...rear end handed to me in there for hurting one of their own, and you're laughing. I have to deal with these people until after your daddy gets home, you know."

She whacked him in the arm with her turtle and laughed again.

Heaven save him from ornery females.

Walking up the sidewalk, he glanced into the front window to see who he might be dealing with. What he saw stopped him in his tracks. Not only was Zoe there, but she was flanked by Claudia, their mother, and May. If ever there was going to be a female ass-whooping, it was going to be now.

Maybe he could just set Phoebe down outside the front door, gesture to Zoe where she was, and then hightail it out of there. Of course that was completely ridiculous, but the thought made him smile and gave him the guts to walk into what could be the equivalent of a hazing.

May said hi first. Claudia followed close behind, with an arched eyebrow and a little more freeze in her words. Zoe's mom waved at him with a small smile, and he had hope this could go okay. But though he waited for Zoe to greet him, or say anything at all, she avoided all eye contact, taking the carrier and turning away.

He couldn't leave like this. While he was certain she would still take care of Phoebe, he didn't want this awkwardness between them.

"Zoe, do you mind giving Phoebe to Claudia, or May, or your mom? I want to talk with you for a minute."

She hesitated, but her shoulders straightened. When she turned around there was that fake smile he had never wanted aimed at him.

"Do you mind, Claudia?" she said as she handed over his niece.

"Not at all. We'll just wait out here. We don't have an appointment for thirty minutes."

It was a subtle warning, but one he got the gist of,

along with Claudia's pursed lips. It said, "Don't upset her." He was going to try not to, but there were some things he couldn't—or wouldn't—change.

Following along behind her through a recessed door, he kept his eyes off her rear end, no matter how difficult it was. If he were free, he would only be thinking about what he could do to her in the time they'd have in the back, how much chaos he could cause in her system in a short amount of time. Instead, he was blocking those thoughts while trying to come up with a way to say what had to be said without feeling like an idiot.

She leaned back against the big desk in the middle of the small room and gestured to one of the sturdy but comfortable-looking visitors' chairs. "Say your piece."

He ran a hand over his hair, not knowing where to start but knowing he had to say something to diffuse the tension thickening the air. "Look, I know I handled the other day badly."

She gave a little snort that could have been in disgust or a short burst of laughter. He had no idea which but had to power on, regardless.

"You do things to me, I admit it. If it were any other time, or a different set of circumstances, you know I would be on you faster than you could take your next breath."

There was a hitch in that next breath, a sign he was not doing this right, or he *was* doing it right, but not for the result he knew he should want—for her to go back to professional and friendly, instead of tempting him to break his own rules.

"I really need you to be here for Phoebe. I can't change how I feel about the best course of action with her. I have to give her my attention and my time. If you and I started anything, I wouldn't be doing that. I'd be jeopardizing the best thing that's come into her life recently."

"Sure." She crossed her arms over that chest he'd dreamed of. She had his own breath hitching, though more quietly.

"Look at how awkward we're being, and all we did is kiss. Can you imagine if we slept together and then you decided you didn't want us anymore? It's not just my own needs I have to think about."

"Why do you keep insisting that I'm going to be that fickle?"

"Come on, Zoe. Even with the pickle jar loosener story, you're still out there looking. I had an idea of what I wanted after Ethan was grown, but Phoebe has to be my priority, and I won't have enough left over to devote to a real relationship. Besides, what happens if you and I break up? What happens to our arrangement and Phoebe? I'm sorry if that's not what you want to hear, but it's the truth."

She unfolded her arms and anchored her hands on the desk next to her hips. "Fine. I'm not saying that's a lie, but it gets confusing when you kissed me like you did and then practically throw me out of the car because I touched you back."

"You're right. That's what I'm apologizing for more than anything else. You're so good with Phoebe. I can't jeopardize that for a few nights in bed that I'm sure would be amazing but in the end would make what we're doing here so much harder. Does that make sense?"

"Yes, in a stupid way it makes sense."

He chuckled at her disgruntled expression. "Believe me, I'm more frustrated than you are, but I know my limits. And being with you would test them, all by itself. Thinking about Ethan still not calling and Phoebe's well-being would push me past the edge."

"Fine, I would like to point out, however, that a lot of people who have kids date, and I think you're being too narrow-minded about this."

"I'll give you that one," he said, relaxing back in the chair. "But it worked for me last time, to some extent. I'm not messing with success until Ethan comes home. That could be months from now. I'm not going to ask you to wait that long."

She sighed. "Fine, but you're missing out on a good thing."

"Believe me, I know." He stuck out a hand. "Friends?"

"Friends," she said grudgingly.

"Thank you." He paused and took her in from head to toe. "No one's going to hand me my ass out there at a later time, are they? I'm pretty tough in court, but I have to say that line of ladies I walked into earlier frightened me."

One side of her mouth quirked up in a smile. "Then we did our job." She punched him in the shoulder. "Now let's get back out there before someone sends a search party, or Claudia decides she's not giving the baby back to me."

This time he led the way out because, for all his talk about being friends, watching her hips sway was a little more than he could take right now.

****

The Phoebster was not having a banner day. She'd

cried and fussed and sniffled. Despite being handed around to everyone on staff, as well as various patrons, no one could get her to turn that sunny smile back on.

"Zoe, if you want to head out with her, you can." Claudia rubbed Phoebe's back.

"I'm nearly done. If you can hang on to her for five more minutes, I'll take her upstairs and see if I can get her down for a nap. Poor thing."

Claudia patted Phoebe's back. "She could be teething. Her bib is sopping with drool."

"She needs a teething ring." She poked around in the diaper bag and came up with one. After handing it over, the baby seemed to calm just a little. She still wasn't happy, though, and Zoe would bet almost anything Dex was going to have a rough night.

Zoe finished up as quickly as possible, then took Phoebe upstairs. Having the apartment above was a great thing. She remembered bringing Justin up here when he wasn't having good days, too. Being right above the shop was a blessing, one she didn't know what she'd do without.

Pacing the floor with Phoebe cradled against her shoulder, she crooned to the little girl while rubbing her back in slow circles. "I wish there was something I could do for you, my angel, but this is part of life."

Phoebe settled in, her crying turning into snuffles. Zoe had given her some liquid pain killer as soon as they came upstairs, and it appeared to finally be working. Once she was certain Phoebe was out, she laid her down in the portable playpen and just looked down at her snuggled in with her turtle. The little girl owned a chunk of her heart. A big chunk, if she were honest, and Dex just might have owned the other part, if she could have convinced him to take a chance on them.

Thinking of him prompted her to text him to let him know he might want to stock up on pain killers and throw some of the teething rings in the fridge to cool them off. She kept her phone on her as she straightened up the living room, then curled up on the couch with a book. He never texted her back. If there was time between Phoebe waking up and when Dex was to arrive, she'd go to the store herself to make sure they wouldn't run out in the middle of the night.

They. Huh. There was no "they" and there wouldn't be for the next eighteen years, if it were up to Dex. She didn't get why he thought it would be easier without a partner, but she did understand being wary. Look at Claudia. She hadn't really dated in the years when Justin was small, and she'd talked about it with Zoe a lot. Not wanting men coming in and out of Justin's life had seemed like the right decision then. But now that it affected her, Zoe couldn't help the disgruntled feeling welling inside her. If he'd just give them a chance, they would make an awesome team. She wasn't afraid of being his pickle jar loosener anymore. At this point she'd almost welcome the risk, if he'd just let her in.

But that was a fairytale ending, and she didn't believe in those. Not for herself, anyway. For other people, sure. May had Brad, Mona had Dad, Claudia had Nate, and Chelsea had snagged Jack at the inn, but those people weren't her and didn't have her track record.

Her phone rang in her hand, and she quickly hit the silence button. Dex was calling. Dex didn't call during the day normally, he just texted to see how things were going.

After peeking over the top of the playpen, Zoe ducked into her room and pulled the door to the frame without actually closing it.

"Hey. What's up?"

"I got a phone call." His voice was flat and the words said in a monotone like announcing that the lunch at school today was Chicken Surprise.

"Okay. Did Ethan tell you he needs more time?"

That got a bark of laughter from him, not at all mirthful, but a harsh impersonation. "If only."

"Then who?"

"Phoebe's grandmother called me at my office about an hour ago and wants to take Phoebe to live with her."

For a moment, she considered the ramifications of that. He'd be free. They'd both be free. But neither of them would have Phoebe or any right to see her, depending on what the grandmother was like.

She was cautious with her next words. "And that would be a bad thing? If Delly's mom wants to take care of her, that might be good in the end, if Ethan never comes back."

"I thought about that for two point one seconds, before I remembered what a horrid woman Delly said she was. And if Delly wanted her to have Phoebe, then why did she come to us?"

Zoe heard the guilt in his voice and then the steel. She went with the next logical question. "How did she get your office number?"

Another mirthless laugh. He was probably pinching the bridge of his nose. "Delly told her where I worked at some point in time, I suppose. She called and demanded for me to be pulled out of a meeting so she could talk to me 'right now.' Donna came to get me because the demand was escalating, and she said the woman threatened legal action if she didn't get me right then. After trying to cajole me into giving her the baby, to no avail, she threatened to take me to court for her. I've just spent my worst fifteen minutes talking to the barracuda who started out pretending to be a guppy."

"Can you get away? Why don't you have Donna reschedule the rest of your day and come over to the apartment? We can talk better when it's not on the phone." She fell back on her bed and drew her knees up.

"I have three more meetings this afternoon. I'll have to take a rain check on the talk, if I even need it at all. What I need is for Ethan to call me. This will not go smoothly if I can't produce the man who has custody of her." His voice was so cold she shivered.

She hadn't even thought of what Ethan being away would mean. This could be a shit storm of epic proportions.

"Why don't you give me Ethan's number, and I'll try calling him? Maybe if it's a different number, he'll pick up out of curiosity."

"No, thanks for offering, but I'll handle this."

Like he'd handled everything else. He was shutting her out, yet again, because it was him against the world. Although she couldn't blame him, it didn't stop the hurt from crawling in on skinned knees.

"Okay, well, we'll be here when you're done. Phoebe's napping, and I'm just hanging, hoping the pain med is working for her poor little mouth. Take whatever time you need."

"Thanks," he said. "I'll text you when I know what time I'll be by for her."

"Okay." She was going to offer to get dinner but thought better of it at the last minute. It was obvious he did not want any interference. It was also a good reminder that, while she was a good nanny for him, it was nothing more than that. They weren't even really friends.

Reality check firmly in place, she said goodbye, went out into the living room, and sat on the couch to watch Phoebe sleep.

Dex might have started out not touching Phoebe a lot, and sometimes she seemed more like a duty than a niece, but he'd been better lately. He would never give her up. Would he?

****

"Shit!" Dex barely held himself back from slamming the phone receiver into the cradle after Zoe said goodbye.

Instead, he put his head in his hands and took deep breath after deep breath. He'd asked Donna to hold any calls until his next meeting. Right now there was nothing more urgent than getting himself back under control and finding a way to get through this minefield.

Dialing the phone, he waited impatiently for Ethan's voicemail to pick up. He was fully aware his brother wouldn't actually answer the damn phone, but he was going to get message after message until he called back.

"You need to call me immediately. I don't care about your precious time or your need to think. If I don't hear from you soon, you're going to lose this baby, and you'll regret it forever. Call me, now, you shit."

He stabbed the off button on the cell phone and then calmly laid it on the desk. He had plans to make and a battle to fight. He'd be damned before he lost a child to a woman who was unfit to have raised her own child. If he had to fight dirty, then he needed all his ducks in a row and not a single webbed foot out of line.

He placed call after call for background checks on Delly's mother and even placed a call to Delly herself. Another voicemail he didn't want to leave, but he had no choice.

Donna announced his next meeting, so he schooled his features into a pleasant and professional mask even as turmoil rode the back of his neck. He would win this, with or without Ethan.

Chapter Fourteen

Six o'clock rolled around, and Zoe paced the floor with Phoebe on her hip as she watched the clock. Most likely Dex would come in, take the baby, and leave. She was trying to prepare herself for that eventuality. She wanted to talk to him, offer him a shoulder, or even just someone to bounce ideas off of. She hadn't forgotten that he didn't want a relationship, or even a date, but that didn't mean she could turn her heart off, no matter how much she would have liked to.

At ten after six the doorbell rang. Zoe smoothed a hand down her shirt, hitched Phoebe up on her hip, and fixed a smile on her face. Hounding him did not strike her as the right thing to do. She admitted she didn't know him very well, but even she knew that.

"Dex." She opened the door wide and stepped back. "I have her all ready to go. Just need to put her in the carrier."

"Thanks." His voice was flat, his expression even flatter.

"Sure." She turned down the fake sunshine a little, since it was obvious it would change nothing and only made her face hurt.

Handing Phoebe to Dex in the carrier, she stepped back, then waited for him to leave. He turned to go, and she couldn't resist offering one more time. "If you need anyone or anything, please don't hesitate to ask."

"Yep. Thanks. See ya." And he was out the door without a backward glance.

Okay then.

Her front door opened, again, and hope fluttered in her chest as she wondered if he'd changed his mind. But it was just Claudia.

"Wow, I just met Dex on the stairs, and he looked ready to kill someone. Did something happen between the two of you?"

Blowing out a breath, Zoe pinched the bridge of her nose before she realized how much that mimicked Dex's frustration. She crossed her arms over her chest, instead. "It's not me, precisely." And she explained what she knew of the new wrinkle in the fabric of Dex's life. More like a major tear.

"See, this is one of the reasons I was so thankful Peter stayed far away, and I was friends with his sister. With May in Justin's life as his biological aunt, this messy stuff never happened."

"I know. Peter might have been a horrible person for walking away from you before you had Justin, but at least we didn't have to deal with this kind of crap." Zoe grabbed a bag of chips from the kitchen, and some dip, along with a bottle of wine.

Claudia settled into a chair in the living room. "So what is Dex going to do? I would think he doesn't have a leg to stand on in court with this thing, not that the grandmother has more rights. But with the one person who has full custody of Phoebe gone, who is legally in charge?"

Zoe plopped on to the couch and dropped the goodies on the coffee table along with two wine glasses. She poured for each of them, then popped open the bag of chips and cracked the lid of the dip.

"I have no idea. Dex is trying to get hold of him, but who knows where he is, or how long it would take for him to get back here."

"Dex has no clue?"

"None. And that's all the info I have because he doesn't want to talk about it and doesn't want any help." She took a healthy swig of her wine. He wasn't going to need her tonight for anything, so it wasn't like she had to be able to drive.

"Yikes, I sense some hostility. I thought you didn't want to get involved, didn't want to be the pickle jar loosener."

Zoe snorted a disgusted laugh. "I'm tired of hearing about the pickle jar thing. I was willing to take a chance on this one being different, but I totally got put in my place on the phone, so I don't think it's an issue anymore."

Zoe found her hand in Claudia's and looked down at their entwined fingers over the rim of her wine glass.

"Don't give up that easily, sweetie."

"It can't be giving up if you hadn't even started to try."

"Now you're being sulky." Claudia sat back on her chair and cocked an eyebrow.

"I'm not being sulky; I'm being realistic. I even offered one last time as he was leaving, and he gave me three short words. Nothing bad at all, but still obvious that he did not want to talk about it, especially with me."

Claudia set her wine glass down and took Zoe's from her. "Have you thought about the fact that with his background and his total lack of long-term relationships, except with his brother, that he might not know how to share this with you?"

Zoe massaged her temples. "I guess that's possible."

"I think it's probable, Zoe. Give the guy the benefit of the doubt. He's been saddled with a kid, a cute kid, an adorable one, but this was not his life plan, and he doesn't have anyone to help him twenty-four hours a day like I did. You were such a lifesaver with Justin, and I know you're helping now, but it's not the same."

"I know that."

"Then know, too, that even with twenty-four-hour help it's hard. And now he has a threat coming in. I didn't have anything like that, but I can imagine what it would have felt like if Peter, or his family, had decided they wanted Justin all for themselves. I'm so thankful I never had to send him to anyone else's house for the weekend, or decide which holidays I could have him for. Dex might not be the most affectionate of people with Phoebe, but you can tell he loves her. This must be like before, with Ethan."

Zoe had shared with Claudia the whole history there. What was this doing to Dex? Was he willing to fight for another child who wasn't his? She would have torn down the world to get Justin if something had happened to Claudia, but she had no real idea what Dex was going through. She'd tried asking, but maybe she should have demanded and made him see they were a team, and a good one.

"He might be relieved to get his life back." She had to voice it, even if she didn't think it was completely true. Then she shook her head. "No, I don't think so. I think he'd die a little inside if they took her away from him now that she belongs to him. She might be his brother's kid, but she's his, and I have a feeling that when someone belongs to Dexter Zegray, it's for a lifetime."

The way Justin belonged to her. The way Dex belonged to her. This was nothing like the surface relationships Zoe had had previously. And though she didn't know all his past, like when he lost his first tooth, or what mischief he had gotten into when he was young, she still had to admit that she knew him. He'd fight with his last breath, with or without Ethan.

"Speaking of Justin…" While they were here she might as well air everything she needed to. "I know you don't want to share him, but can I have him some weekends?"

Claudia grabbed Zoe's hands. "Yes." She pulled her in for a hug. "This whole conversation just reminded me that I took Justin from you without a single thought, and he's as much yours as he is mine. I'm sorry, sweetie."

Zoe's eyes misted up. "No need to apologize. I should have said something earlier. I just was so happy that you were happy that I didn't want to burden you with it."

"Hell, what else is family for if not to burden?" She let Zoe go and smiled. "And with that, I'm going to burden you again."

"With what?"

"A secret you can't tell anyone yet."

Zoe sat forward. It must be big, if Claudia prefaced it like that. "What?"

"Well, it seems you are going to have to be both maid of honor and new auntie soon."

"Come again?"

Claudia smiled. "Nate managed to knock me up, so we're moving the wedding along quickly. The baby will be here in six months. Think we can fit it all in?"

"Oh, my God, yes!" She went to Claudia for a fierce hug. "It won't be the same, raising a child without my stellar input."

Claudia pulled away, wiping her eyes. "Who says you're not going to have a hand in this? You're getting her when she cries."

Zoe laughed out, loud and long, wiping her eyes, too. Things had changed, but that didn't mean some parts wouldn't be even better this time. She had a lot to be hopeful for. And that made her think of Dex. He was going against a wall by himself, and he shouldn't have to. Even if she had to force him to listen to her, she was going to let him know he was not alone.

"It's seven o'clock, and I had one sip of wine. Should I go to him now?"

"I'd let him have the night. Talk to him tomorrow. Tonight, you and I are going to stay up for hours, talk, watch movies, order pizza, and have fun. Nate knows I'm not coming home. He and Justin are having guy time. It's just you and me, sweets. Think you can handle that?"

"Absolutely. Tomorrow is early enough to beard that particular dragon."

****

"She's only responding to your stress," Dex said for the fifth time, like a mantra. He couldn't get Phoebe to calm down enough to go to sleep. He'd tried the gum gel and rubbing her back. He'd walked up and down the second floor hall so much he was sure there was a rut in the carpet. Nothing worked.

A new wave of crying came on, and he was about to break down and join her. Picking up her and her turtle from the crib, he tried walking, again. The lure of calling Zoe was incredible. She would probably know what to do to help Phoebe calm down. If nothing else, she wouldn't be so tense, every muscle in her body coiled, like his currently were. But he'd already told her he was going to do this alone, and he would.

Phoebe wasn't calming down. He was running out of options, and it was midnight. The morning would come soon and yet would probably feel like it took forever if he couldn't get her to stop crying. Walking downstairs, he decided to wear a path in the carpet between the living room and family room. He needed new scenery, if nothing else.

On one pass, a mound of tools caught his eye in the corner of the little-used dining room. He hadn't thought of the piece of furniture under that pile in years. It was simply a catch-all for things Ethan used but didn't ever put away. Now it could be his savior.

He used his free hand to clear tool chests and brown boxes of hinges and other small pieces from the rocking chair, then stood back. His mother had supposedly rocked Ethan in this chair, though Dex didn't have any real memories of her doing anything that maternal.

Regardless, it would be used now. Grabbing a blanket from the living room, he placed it on the oak seat and draped it over the spindle he didn't want digging into his back.

After arranging Phoebe in the crook of his arm, he sat and gently set the chair to rocking. A lullaby popped into his head, the one about the cradle falling from the tree. He did his best to sing it, even if his voice wasn't going to get him into any karaoke bars.

A few snuffles later, the little girl gave a big sigh and fell into blessed sleep. He didn't care if his bladder burst, or the apocalypse came, he was not moving from this spot until morning.

Not moving gave him time to think, though, too much time to think. Was he going about this wrong? Sure, he had raised Ethan alone, but Ethan had also been twelve, not six months old. And with Ethan he'd never had anyone offer to help. How much easier could it have been if he had had help? If it hadn't just been him and Ethan against the world?

It wouldn't have been easy, no matter how many people he'd had, but it could have been less stressful if spread out. He couldn't change the past, but he could make the future different. If he had the courage to trust her. And the ability to let go of complete control.

His eyes drifted closed on that thought. He didn't know if he'd be able to do that, but he might need to try. Delly's mom could be a lot harder than a state system who hadn't really wanted Ethan but thought Dex shouldn't have him either.

He was almost asleep, thinking that perhaps he should move them to the couch so he didn't drop her in his sleep, when his phone rang.

Who would be calling him at three o'clock in the morning? As quickly as he could, he put Phoebe on the couch and tucked pillows around her, then grabbed his phone from the dining room table.

He jabbed the answer button a second before it would have gone to voicemail and greeted Delly in the nicest voice he could manage for the woman who had started this avalanche but who had also given him one of the most important people in his life.

"Damn, I was hoping to leave a message," she said after his hello.

"Well, we all want things we can't have." He pinched the bridge of his nose. "If you want to pretend this is voicemail, then go for it. What message would you like to leave?"

"I don't need your attitude."

"And I don't need to be the only one caring for a child who's been abandoned by both parents. Life's not exactly fair, is it?"

"Where's Ethan?" Her panic rang through the phone. "When he left here two days ago, he said he was going home."

"Ethan came to you?" he demanded. Why the hell would he have gone there?

"Yes, he came to see me because he was... It doesn't matter. I told him to go home."

Dex let out a sigh of equal parts exhaustion and frustration. What the hell was going through that boy's head? "Well, he didn't make it." Dex was ready to panic because Ethan hadn't shown up, whether due to an accident or something else terrible. He couldn't think about that right now, though. He had enough going on, and on the phone he had the mother of the finally sleeping infant. He just had to keep his cool while he got some answers out of her.

"Why are you being such an ass?" she asked, all belligerence.

He huffed out a laugh at that one. "Really, Delly? I'm being an ass? I've been up with a crying baby who just went to sleep after three hours of walking and fifteen minutes of rocking. I'm exhausted, and you choose to call in the middle of the night in hopes of leaving me a voicemail. Should I hang up? I can put the phone on vibrate and let you call back."

"She likes the rocking best," Delly said quietly with a hitch in her voice.

His heart beat a little harder. This did not sound like the Delly who had left in a rush over two weeks ago without a backward glance.

"What happened, Delly?"

"I don't want to talk about it. I'll leave that message now."

There was a full minute of silence. "Go ahead," he said, closing his eyes.

"Don't let my mother take the baby. She just wants you to pay child support to her if she gets Phoebe." There was that hitch again on her daughter's name. "I'll send you a letter or something, explaining that I don't want her to have Phoebe, no matter what, but that's the best I can do. And if Ethan shows up here again, I'll tell him to go home." Then dead silence as she hung up on her end.

He returned to the living room to make sure Phoebe was still sleeping, then sat down on the opposite side of the couch. While a letter might help some, it wasn't going to be easy to use it when the writer no longer had any legal rights to the child in question and the father was gone, leaving Dex with a bundle to carry that was really not his in any legal manner.

Resting his head back against the couch, he ran over all the possibilities and all the ways this could go. None of them were good, but he'd make the best of it, as he always did.

He left another message for Ethan before he curled around Phoebe on the couch and slept. Tomorrow would be better. It had to be.

Chapter Fifteen

Zoe was up at dawn and down in Decadence making flower arrangements by seven. She hadn't slept well last night, even with Claudia in her old bedroom. They'd laughed and talked and had a great time, but this situation with Dex had sat at the back of her mind the whole time.

How was she going to force him to talk to her? She was a big believer in letting people work things out for themselves, if possible. It was one of the things Justin had told her he liked best about her when he was younger—that she was there to listen but didn't press like other people did. However, that might not be the solution this time, and she had to figure out how to do this differently.

By nine she had expected to see Dex, but he hadn't shown up yet. She thought about going to get him, again, but a slew of orders came in for a funeral, and she didn't surface again until ten-thirty.

"Claudia, I'm going to see what's up with Dex," she called out as she removed her apron and hung it on the hook in the back room.

"Use your charm to get him to talk, Zoe. Don't be bristly."

"I'm never bristly," she said in a huff.

Claudia just looked at her, making Zoe sigh.

"Fine, I'll behave, but he is going to talk to me."

"I don't doubt it."

"I'll be back in a half hour at the most." She took her light jacket from the hook beside her apron and put it on.

"I don't think there's anything more to do here right now, and orders can wait, for something this important."

"Thanks." She smiled and kissed Claudia on the cheek. "Wish me luck."

"I don't think you're going to need it," Claudia said, looking over her shoulder at something in the front of the store.

Zoe turned to find a haggard-looking Dex toting Phoebe's carrier in from the car. Stubble covered the lower half of his face and his eyes looked hollow.

"Emergency boy-girl meeting," Zoe murmured as she made eye contact with Claudia.

Thankfully her sister knew exactly what she needed without her uttering another word. She took the carrier from Dex and gave him a gentle shove in Zoe's direction as she walked away.

Dex stumbled forward, and Zoe caught him by the arm, using his momentum to propel him right into the office at the back of the store. They were having this conversation, and they were having it now.

"Sit," she said, plopping him into the comfortable guest chair before circling the desk to take a seat herself.

With his hand over his eyes, he sighed. After a moment his blue-eyed gaze locked in on hers. "I don't have time for this."

"You're going to make time for this." She picked up the phone and dialed. "Hey, Donna, I'm holding Dex hostage here at Decadence. Does he have anything that he needs to be there for at the moment?"

"No, he's free until noon," the other woman said. "Or he will be as soon as we hang up. Talk some sense into that man, Zoe. I know you can do it."

"Will do. Give my love to Uncle Al." She hung up and folded her hands in front of her on the desk. "You're free until noon. Now start talking."

Dex sat up straighter in his chair. "I don't have time for this, and I don't have anything to say."

"Sure you do, for both. And I'll warn you that emergency meetings are only for the highest order of bullshit, and I'm calling bullshit. Now, talk to me, or we'll be in here until doomsday."

The stare-down nearly broke her heart as she looked into his bloodshot eyes. "Bend, Dex. Please. I'm not asking you to break, or hand over everything. I'm just asking for you to bend, give me a little. I can help."

The look he gave her was a combination of resignation and a smidgen of hope. She'd talk until she was blue in the face and lock the door if necessary.

When he didn't say anything to her offer, she trucked on anyway. "I've been thinking about this, and I'm sure you have most of it handled already, and your argument totally planned out, with cases cited and law jargon quoted. I'm sure you have the whole thing laid out, but have you shared it with anyone?"

"No."

"Why not me? I don't have a big part in this, but I do have somewhat of a stake. Why won't you talk?"

"Is this going to be one of those stereotypical 'we need to talk' conversations? I don't have time for that."

"You know what? It was going to be, but now it's

going to be something a whole lot worse." She rose from the chair to perch on the edge of the desk, almost in his face.

He crossed his arms over his chest, and she wanted to punch him.

"What in the hell is wrong with not always going it alone, you jerk?" She poked him in the chest. "I'm fine if you don't want to have a relationship with me. I understand the reasoning, even if I don't agree with it. But this is bigger, and you're shutting me out. I deserve better than that. You brought me in to help you with Phoebe, but then you keep me at arm's length when I try to do anything else. You want a nanny? I can be that, but I'm more than that, too. Don't expect me to just forget about the two of you when she leaves for the day. I already have a job. This is more about loving that little girl than it is about making your life more comfortable." She crossed her own arms over her chest. "You have a lot more going on than one person should have to go through alone. I'm not asking for you to ask me to help you, as that might be more than you'd be capable of. I'm asking you to simply accept what I'm giving freely."

He stood from his chair. She was afraid she was going to have to chase him through the store. Instead, he engulfed her in a hug, his full frame wrapped around hers and his lips in her hair.

"I would appreciate it," he said, low but loud enough for it to reach her ears.

"You would?"

"Yes. Can you take tomorrow afternoon off? I have a meeting with the grandmother then, and I'd like to not be alone. I was going to ask you to watch the Phoebster, but I'll ask Jack and Chelsea to keep her at the inn, instead. I don't want the grandmother anywhere near Phoebe."

"Done."

****

"Are you sure you don't mind?" Dex asked Chelsea the next afternoon. He'd never have imagined he'd have so many people wrapped up in this issue. Not only had he accepted Zoe's help, but now he was imposing on Jack and Chelsea, who had an inn to run and a precocious four-year-old to keep track of.

"It's our pleasure, Dex, so stop asking that." Chelsea took Phoebe and the turtle into her arms, then bent down to introduce the two to her daughter Mazzy.

"She's perfect!" Mazzy said, clapping her hands. "Like a doll, Mommylove! I love her! I hold her right now?"

"In a minute, sweetie. You'll have to sit on the couch to hold her. Let's say goodbye to Zoe and Dex, and then we'll go into the sitting room."

"Bye! Bye! Bye!" Mazzy yelled before running into the next room.

Chelsea smiled after her daughter. "I'm sure she'd like to visit with you, too, but just not right now when there's a new special something to do."

"No worries," Zoe said. She hugged Chelsea as Dex stood back. "We'll be back soon, hopefully."

"Shouldn't be more than an hour." Dex shoved his hands into his pants pockets. It would be a shorter time, if he could make that happen.

"No rush. I'm sure we'll have a blast with her. And she's good practice for when Jack and I decide to add to our family."

They took their leave, Dex's hands still in his pockets. He didn't want to spend all day with his arms crossed, yet he didn't know what else to do to still his nervous fingers.

"This is just a preliminary," he said when they got into his car. He didn't look at her as he turned the ignition or when they pulled out of the driveway. However, he was sure she was looking at him with that light in her eyes that did something to his chest. She was going to be fierce in the meeting, he just knew it. As fierce as she had been yesterday before he'd hugged her. And he loved her for it.

He almost jammed his foot on the brake when that thought came in and blindsided him. He caught himself at the last second. There was no time to think about the revelation because they'd pulled up in front of the law offices of Timothy McCrane, Esq.

"I'm going to follow your lead in there, and I'm really just here for support," she said, laying her hand over his. "This is your show, your niece, but I'm right there if I think you need something."

"Thanks."

"Not so hard, is it?"

"I wouldn't go that far, but I appreciate you being here. Let's go take the thorn out of the lion's paw."

She laughed, and he felt a smile crack on his face.

After being escorted through the warren of offices, they arrived at Timothy's door. He and Dex had had some dealings over the last year, and Dex had found him fair and just. Hopefully that would happen when they weren't on the same side, too.

He knocked. Timothy called out for him to enter.

He opened the door and let Zoe go in first. She

chose the seat in the middle of the room, leaving the last chair for him by the door. While he appreciated her seat choice, he could have handled sitting next to Cathy Ferndale.

"Let's get the introductions out of the way and then get down to business," Timothy said.

They did just that before Cathy started in with the crocodile tears. "I thought the baby would be here." She held a handkerchief up to her narrowed eyes.

"I thought it best to have this first meeting without her here. That way we can concentrate on what's best for her."

"I'm what's best for her. She lived with me for the first five months of her life. I love her and should be taking care of her if my daughter won't." The handkerchief remained at her face, hiding from Timothy's view the frown and her puckered mouth.

"Only five months? I thought the child was six months old." Timothy stepped right in, and Dex's hope rose.

"Well, yes, um, she was with me for the full six months until Delilah took her away and gave her to the father...who also seems to be missing. And yet we have this woman here who I don't know." Her fists clenched in her lap, the handkerchief forgotten in her indignation.

"Zoe has been caring for Phoebe for the last few weeks. I wanted her backing on this meeting. Ethan is not here because, again, I did not want to expose him to you before we settled a few things." A lie, but one he was betting she wasn't going to be able to refute.

The handkerchief got mangled at his words. "I'm not someone you have to hide everyone from. I love that little girl. She should be with someone who loves her."

Wasn't it curious that the woman wouldn't say her name?

"Phoebe deserves to be with her father, not her grandmother. Although I use that term lightly," he said. Zoe put her hand on the arm of his chair, not quite touching him but definitely there for him.

"How dare you!"

"I dare because it's true, Mrs. Ferndale. A little digging into your background shows me that you've never had a child. Delly is actually your deceased sister's daughter who you took on and immediately quit your job to live on food stamps and state aid after that. Well, at least until she finally left your house about two months ago." He leaned forward in his chair to make eye contact with her. "Are you sure Phoebe lived with you for her whole life until she came to my house?"

Her hackles went up. He could almost see steam coming out of her ears. If he could get her to lose her composure, his case for keeping the little girl away from her would be made for him.

But she cleared her throat and brought the handkerchief back to her eyes. "I didn't want Delly to go. I asked her to please let Ethan know he had a daughter, because he might want to be a part of her life, but she refused and left, taking my darling granddaughter with her."

"I highly doubt that, and I don't even know you," Zoe mumbled.

"Who the hell are you in all this? His floozy? I don't want my granddaughter raised in sin with the two of you going at each other every second of the day in front of her young eyes!"

She was getting closer to losing it. But until she lost it over something that didn't make him look bad, he wasn't going to win.

"Zoe is the nanny and takes care of Phoebe during the day."

"I could take care of her all day long without needing to hire an outsider."

He wanted to ask if she was going to apply for food stamps again, then. So many people were truly in need of that kind of assistance and worked hard but just didn't make ends meet. For those people he would gladly buy the groceries himself, but this woman was taking advantage of the system and taking away from those who could really use its help.

He stopped himself and instead went for his ace in the hole to rock her boat. "And what about what Delly wants? I have here a letter from her that she faxed me this morning, asking in the strongest terms to please not give the baby to you." He handed a copy to Timothy and another to Cathy. "She might not have legal rights to the child. However, I believe her opinion should be weighed fairly. She gave Phoebe to Ethan instead of you. That says something, too."

He watched Cathy's eyes track from left to right over and over again as she read the damning letter from Delly detailing the way her mother had kicked her out for not going after Dex and Ethan for child support. How she had never even held Phoebe when they lived there, much less watched her. She'd forced Delly to ask her friends to watch the baby, or give away over half her paycheck to a day care for her longer hours.

He watched for when she got to the part about refusing to let Delly use the car to take Phoebe to the doctor's office when the little girl had an ear infection. The edges of the page crumpled in her hands as her face turned red.

"And let's not forget all those bruises Delly used to sport when she came to our house every day. For some reason she never fell down my stairs, but she often fell down yours."

By this time Timothy had sat back in his office chair and was watching the whole thing play out like a stage drama. The fact that he wasn't making notes of any kind told Dex he'd already made up his mind about something.

"I will not let my niece be raised in a house where she's not loved and cherished for exactly who she is," he said. "If you want to fight me on that, then I'd be happy to see you in court."

"You fucking bastard," Cathy roared as she came out of her chair, hands like claws.

Zoe was just as fast and met her halfway. "Sit the hell down." She towered over Cathy and seemed to grow with every breath. More quietly, and with an edge of violence to it, she repeated herself when Cathy made no move to back up: "Sit the hell down."

Cathy's hand was out like the crack of a whip and made contact with Zoe's cheek before Dex could stop her.

Timothy and Dex both shot out of their chairs and were yelling about the ramifications of that hit. But Zoe put her hand up for silence.

She shook her head. "The first one you get free because maybe you don't know any better, but the next one is going to land you on your ass."

He had no idea what Zoe's face looked like, since

he was behind her, but Cathy sat quickly with fear in her eyes.

"Timothy," Zoe said, turning to face him and laying her hands on his desk. "I don't have a lot to lose here other than the pleasure of seeing a happy girl grow up in a home with love, and I don't know all the laws, even though Uncle Al has tried to teach me a thing or two. But I'd say we're done here. May I have a moment or two with Cathy to see if she feels the same way?"

"I don't know if that's in anyone's best interest." Timothy did not, however, look completely closed to the idea. "Cathy, would you like a moment with Zoe?"

The fire had re-entered the woman's eyes, burning off the fear. "Yes, I believe I would."

"I don't know if this is a good—" Dex started but was cut off by Zoe.

"It's an excellent idea. Trust me."

"I do." He wished she'd turn around so she could see how much he meant those words, but she was laser-focused on Cathy. He rose from the chair and joined Timothy at the office door. "I'll be right outside."

She turned and gave him a smile. "Thank you. We're going to be fine."

He didn't know if she meant her and Cathy, or him and Zoe, but he was hoping for both as he walked through the door and out into the hallway.

Chapter Sixteen

Zoe took an extra breath before she turned to the woman behind her. She noticed the door slightly ajar and immediately knew she would do whatever she had to in order to keep this nasty woman from noticing. "You and I are having an emergency girl meeting, Cathy. It's going to be a quick and dirty one."

The other woman shot a glare at her. "I have nothing to say to you."

"Come on. You wanted this as much as I do. What do you want here?"

"The baby."

"Her name is Phoebe. And you don't really want her. It wouldn't have taken you this many weeks to get her if you really wanted her. You would have found out where Dex lives and gone to his house ready to come to a solution if you really wanted her. So that's not it." She tapped her lips, pretending to think. "No, I think you want the easy way."

"I've never had the easy way. You don't even know how hard it's been, bitch."

"We don't need to resort to name calling. I have a choice few you aren't going to want to hear." She paced behind the desk. "I don't know how hard it's been, but I do know that you're trying to take something from Dex that he doesn't want to give up. So what would you take in exchange?"

A light came into Cathy's eyes. Zoe knew she had hit pay dirt. Literally.

"How much would it take for you to walk away?" Zoe asked. "Give me a round figure. I own my own florist shop, and I make quite a bit of money. Dex is a successful lawyer. What would it take to make you walk away?"

One side of Cathy's mouth curled up. "You're smarter than I would have given you credit for."

"Name it."

"Two hundred thousand." Cathy Ferndale crossed her legs and settled back into the chair. "Two hundred thousand, and this can all go away. You can set up house with Dex, and the two of you can raise the crying brat until she becomes a screaming teenager that you didn't want in the first place."

Zoe's heart clenched at the thought of being able to raise Phoebe with Dex. They'd make her a family she would never regret. "Two hundred thou. That's kind of steep."

"Take it, or I take you to court," Cathy demanded.

"Or we can take you to court," Timothy said from the doorway. "You might want to make sure the door is all the way closed before you start making back alley bargains for children who aren't yours."

Cathy screamed in frustration and headed out the door at full speed. She banged into the wall across the hallway before righting herself and running.

"Are we just going to let her go?" Dex asked as he took Zoe's hand in his.

"I don't think there's much we could do to her as long as she doesn't bring suit against you." Timothy resumed his seat at the desk. "You'd make a mean negotiator, Zoe Bradley. Your uncle is some kind of teacher."

Zoe laughed. "Oh, he never actually taught me anything. That's called schoolyard tactics, in my book. As long as it worked, I'm good with that."

"Me, too." Dex brought her hand to his mouth and kissed the back of her knuckles.

Something sparked in his eyes, something she hadn't seen in a while—lust. Her insides quivered at the intent in his gaze. If he could do that with a look, what would he be able to accomplish with his hands?

Totally inappropriate thought for a lawyer's office with no privacy, but she let it linger long enough in her own eyes to show Dex she wasn't afraid of what he wanted.

"Well, that took considerably less time than I had expected," Timothy said, breaking the sexual tension straining between them.

"Yes," Dex said, turning to the lawyer while still keeping Zoe's hand in his. "Thank you. I'm sorry it got ugly."

"Hey, it's all part of the job, you know that. See you next week for poker?"

"If things are more settled then, yes. I'll keep you posted, and let me know if Cathy tries to stir up more trouble."

"Will do. You know your way out." And they lost him to paperwork.

Zoe pulled him out to the car so she could hug him properly without witnesses.

"Yes!" She pumped her fist in the air as he unlocked her door first. She threw her arms around his neck and went in for a hug. He, however, had a different intention and pushed her up against the car as he took utter and complete possession of her mouth.

She sighed when he stopped plundering her mouth long enough to kiss her neck and that sensitive spot on her earlobe.

"My apartment is close."

"But you have people working downstairs. My house is clear."

"Take me there?"

"Yes."

They held hands but didn't talk. The anticipation was smothering every word she wanted to utter.

She had his shirt off before he even made it all the way across the threshold. She pulled him into the house by the tie lying loose around his throat and slammed the door behind him. Then she pressed his body up against the door and had her way with his mouth.

"Good God," Dex said, panting when they finally came up for air.

But Zoe wasn't in the mood for talk. She wanted more action, and she wanted it now. She sealed her lips to his as she dragged him up to his bedroom with the tie still around his neck. She might even let him keep it on, in case it would come in handy later.

While she backed him up the stairs, she nibbled, licked, and moaned her way down his throat. His knees finally hit the edge of the mattress, and she tumbled him onto the bed, ending up straddled over his lap.

"I'd like to protest now that you are taking advantage of me." He grinned and made her heart beat faster.

"You love it."

"And I love—holy freaking Mary mother of God."

She gave him a wicked smile and admired the way her hand encircled him. And if it had the added bonus of keeping the encounter light and hot and sexy, instead of deep and utterly romantic, then so much the better for her.

Not much talking happened for a while other than sighs and moans with a couple of "yes" words thrown in for a mix. With his hands and teeth and body, Dex took Zoe to higher heights than she'd ever known, even in her previous encounters with him. He played her like an accountant with his favorite big adding machine. His fingers ran a staccato of numbers over her ribs and up to her nipples. His tongue delved into her, onto her, and nearly left her weeping.

She returned the favor by caressing him, learning the planes and angles of his body in her frenzy to get him inside her at the absolute earliest opportunity.

But then he slowed and seemed to savor. She was about to go off like a bottle rocket and he was taking his damn sweet time. Men! She knew how to get him going, though. So she slid down his body with the grace of a python and zeroed in on her target.

"Now." She ran a fingernail over the length of him and had him groaning. As slowly as she could, with her hands trembling and her breath coming in short pants, she raised her knees to make a place for him.

Her mouth was watering just thinking about getting to all that hard flesh that could make her scream like a free fall on a huge roller coaster. But then she looked into his eyes and he was doing that thing where he stared into her soul. He gripped her hands tightly as he entered her, mesmerizing her with the sweet ache of his size and weight and the bliss of having him connect with her both physically and emotionally. He might regret this later, so she'd take it for all she was worth now.

****

When Dex had kissed Zoe against his car he knew their time together would be phenomenal. He hadn't quite anticipated how lost he would be in the scent and the feel of her. Her skin was like rose petals, her lips all consuming, her touch like a balm. And all of it combined to make him lost in her.

He lay next to her, holding her hand as they both worked to calm their breathing. "I was wrong," he said.

She squeezed his fingers. "About what?"

"There's no way once is going to be enough."

She laughed, a breathy sound that made him hard again.

"We have to go get Phoebe soon, Dex. It'll have to be enough."

He turned on his side and waited for her to look at him. "Will you stay tonight?"

She got two little lines between her eyebrows. "I'm not sure that's a good idea."

"It's a brilliant idea." He kissed her palm. "That's the other thing I was wrong about. I don't want to do this alone. I never would have been able to achieve what you did today without making myself look like an asshole. I want to be that team you talk about." He kissed her cheek. "Will you stay?"

Turning, she faced him fully, her lush body a temptation for him all over again. She placed a palm against his cheek. "Yes, I'll stay."

He kissed her on the lips, then gave her a light slap on her butt. "We'd better go get our girl, then. We can order some pizza or something in celebration of a couple different things." He winked at her and left her in the bed as he went to get dressed.

Being scared and being alone had not been the way to do this. He got that now. Thank goodness it was before he'd pushed her away completely.

****

Waking up in Dex's arms was an experience she'd love to have every single day. She stretched a full body stretch, letting every part of her touch every part of him. He smiled with his eyes still closed and kissed her when she met him halfway.

"She slept all night," she said, cuddling into him.

"Must have been because most of the tension left the house after yesterday." He rubbed her back with slow sure strokes, making her want to stretch again like a cat. "Did I thank you for yesterday? All of it?"

Giggling, she put her hand on his heart. "Yes, I think I was sufficiently thanked."

"Should I just get you a card next time?" He cracked one eye open.

Now she laughed full out. "Don't you dare!"

Rolling over until he was braced above her and staring down into her eyes, he brushed her bangs off her forehead. "I really do appreciate everything you did."

She ran her palm over his cheek. "I know. You're the only one I've ever wanted to take someone on for. I hope I never have to do that again, though."

A little kiss on her nose tickled. "I hope it is never necessary again." He dropped his forehead to hers. "I do have to say that I'm almost thankful for Cathy's attitude and mercenary bent."

She followed when he rolled back over, stacking

167

her hands on his chest. "Why do you say that?"

"I thought giving Phoebe a roof and three meals a day might be all I could do, but I love that little girl, and I'll do right by her. Look at how Delly grew up without someone to love her. I won't do that to Phoebe. She wiggled her way into my heart. I can't imagine not having her."

She placed a kiss below his nipple. She wouldn't tell him that there was still a possibility that Phoebe could be taken away. If Ethan got himself together and came back and found someone to make a life with, there was every possibility that they would move out to make that life, too. Dex would be relegated to uncle status just like she had been demoted to being only an aunt.

Then again, Claudia had said she could have Justin some days. Perhaps it was simply a matter of asking. They'd have that discussion much later, though, if ever.

"No thinking when you're naked and in my bed. It's a rule." Dex nudged her knee with his leg and she opened for him under the cover of the sheets. They'd hear Phoebe through the intercom if she woke up.

Dex traced a path down under the sheet, making her shiver.

Things were heating up and she was about to ascend straight to heaven when the door to the bedroom banged open. Zoe yanked the sheet up to her chin and yelped just as the man in the doorway said, "Hello, brother, maybe you don't need me after all."

Chapter Seventeen

"I'll meet you downstairs in five minutes." Dex stayed right where he was in the big bed, warm from Zoe. He did not want to jump naked out of bed, but he couldn't take the sheet with him to stand, since that would leave Zoe bare.

"Right," Ethan said with several layers of nasty in his voice. "I busted my ass to get back here, and you're banging some chick while my daughter is in the next room. Classy. Shall we have brunch to go with the class?"

"Get out now, Ethan, and close your mouth while you close the damn door. I will be right there."

The snicker Ethan left with was malice incarnate.

"I should go," Zoe said, jumping out of bed and grabbing her clothes from where they'd both thrown them last night.

"You're as much a part of this as I am, now. You can go if you want, I won't stop you, but I'd like you here."

That stopped her. She turned with her clothes against her chest and eyes wide. "Are you sure?"

"Yes, we're in this together now." He took the sheet with him when he got out of bed. "Get dressed and grab Phoebe, if you don't mind. Meet me down in the kitchen. It's where all Zegray meetings are held. I'll put on coffee and get things started with a lecture about not being rude to people who are important to me. Then we'll segue into Phoebe when you come down." He kissed her on the mouth and shooed her into the bathroom before he yanked on a pair of jeans and a T-shirt. Ethan could just deal with messy hair.

As he walked down the stairs, he concentrated on regulating his blood pressure and practiced what he'd say to the boy who had left when the going got tough only to come back and demand answers.

If he thought yesterday was tough, this was going to make Cathy look like a fluffy cat circus.

He took one last breath before he entered the kitchen. Ethan was banging cabinets and the fridge open and shut. He could have his tantrum later.

"Sit the hell down and knock it off."

"That's rich. You want to tell me why the hell I should listen to you?"

"Because your daughter is upstairs in the care of a woman who has helped me since your ass left town in the middle of the night. Neither of them are going to come down to you having a temper tantrum."

They stared at each other across the kitchen. Dex was not going to back down. He'd stand here for the rest of the day if he had to.

It didn't take that long, however. Ethan threw himself into a chair with his arms crossed and his mule expression on his face. At least it was better than banging things around.

"Now," Dex said, and he seated himself across the kitchen table from the sulking hulk. "Let's start over. Where have you been?"

"That's none of your damned business. It's enough that I'm back. Delly told me I had to come home because something was brewing. So here I am, and I get to walk in on you screwing. Rhymes, but it's not quite the same thing, is it?"

Dex held onto his temper by a thread. "I was not screwing." Ethan snorted. "Look, that part of my life is none of your damned business, if we're drawing lines. I've been taking care of your daughter for two weeks while you did who knows what. I'm the one who gets to ask the questions."

"Fire away. I'm not answering anything. I will tell you this, though—I want her out of the house. We don't need some broad muddling things up. I'm back now. We don't need her."

"Of course we're going to need her. And even if we didn't, I want her here and this is my house."

"Fine, then I'll take off again."

"And are you taking Phoebe with you, Ethan?" He tented his hands on the table's surface. "Because I'll fight you tooth and nail. I've already fought for Sam to keep your job open. I've also paid all your bills so you still have insurance and the freaking phone you never answered. And I fought Delly's mother. I'm not afraid to take you on."

Sullenly silent, Ethan just sat there.

"You don't have anything to say? No wondering how your daughter is doing, or what hell I've been through since you snuck out?"

"I'm not supposed to ask questions, remember. So I guess I'll just sit here while you make all the decisions for my life and tell me how to raise my daughter, since I obviously know nothing."

Dex blew out a breath and pinched the bridge of his nose. Christ, this was torture.

"Let's start over for the third time."

"I don't want to start over. I want to finish this." Ethan jammed his hands onto the tabletop. "You want the baby? Fine, you raise her. I thought it was you and me against the world, though, and now you're dropping me for a bitch."

"He's not dropping you, you ungrateful brat," Zoe said in a sweet voice as she entered the kitchen with a sunny Phoebe on her hip. When they walked fully into the tension-filled kitchen, Phoebe's face screwed up.

"Don't cry, sweetie," Dex said, getting up and taking her from Zoe. "Do you mind getting her a bottle?"

"Not at all," she said.

"Well, isn't this just the absolute picture of domesticity? You're so cute together. What the hell do you need me for? I'll sign her over to you and be on my way. And all will be well."

"What are you talking about? You are not going to walk out on this child again." Dex sat at the table and let Phoebe play with a napkin. Continuously taking it out of her mouth for her to put back in was a game she loved to play.

"It was always you and me against the world, Dex, but now you have the two females, so I'll just move on."

"That's ridiculous. She needs you; you're her father."

"No, I'm not. It takes more than genetics to make a father, you taught me that, and now you're teaching me that you'll do a better job than I ever would." He rose from the chair. "My car's still packed. I'll call if I think about it."

Dex thrust Phoebe back at Zoe and followed him out of the house, slamming his hand on the car door when Ethan went to unlock it. "Are you fucking kidding me?"

"No, I'm not." Ethan stabbed the key in the lock again, and Dex whipped the keys out of his hand.

"Get back in that house, and we're going to talk about this like adults. The time for messing around is over, Ethan. You have a little girl in there who needs you. I gave you your free time. It's over now."

"And what if that's not what I want?" Ethan stepped back with hatred in his eyes.

"I don't care anymore what you want. I care about what Phoebe needs, and she needs you."

Ethan pinched the bridge of his nose, making Dex wonder at how alike they were. That's why he was demanding Ethan stay. He needed to know this was bigger than either one of them, and he was not leaving. Nineteen might be young to care for a baby, but people that age did it all the time.

"I don't want *her* here, then. Give me that in exchange for me not leaving. You want to bang her at her house, or take her out for a night on the town, fine. But this is my house, too, and I don't want to be invaded by some do-gooder you're getting cozy with."

Dex took that like a physical blow. "What is wrong with you? You've never talked about women like this before."

"Yeah, and I've never caught you in bed with one before, so I guess we're both new to this. Get her out, and I'll come back in."

"I'll ask her to leave, but you're going to show some respect. She has been nothing but helpful since I asked her to watch Phoebe. You don't have to talk to her, but if you're going to, it's going to be with respect."

And it was a small price to pay. Zoe would understand that he and Ethan needed time together. He didn't want to have to choose between them, but this would be a temporary thing until he explained to Ethan how important Zoe was to him.

"Get your first load together. I'll have her out in a minute. Then you and I are talking, until I'm hoarse if I have to."

Heading back into the house, he found Zoe right in the kitchen where he'd left her.

"Is this going to be ugly when he comes back in?" She rocked from side to side with Phoebe, the turtle and the bottle all tucked in close.

"Actually, I'm going to take care of this round, so it won't be ugly for you. I told him he should be grateful to you instead of hateful, but if I know him, he's going to be stubborn. I don't want to put you through that. Why don't you hand Phoebe over and head out? I'll call you tonight after I get things settled, and let you know how it went."

"You're shutting me out again." She hunched her shoulders in, and it made him sad even though it didn't change his mind.

"I'm sorry, Zoe. I'm not shutting you out, but I need to do this on my own. I promise I'll call you tonight."

"Okay." She handed the baby over. Phoebe smelled of powder and clothes soap, and it made his heart glad to sniff at her. She was the reason all this was happening, and he'd do right by her, no matter the cost.

Dex kissed Zoe on the cheek when he walked her to the front door. "I'll talk some sense into him."

"Good luck with that. I'll talk to you tonight."

"You got it."

She kissed Phoebe on the head and then him on the cheek. He watched her walk to her car, taking his last easy breath for some time.

****

Zoe filled her night with making plans on how they could all integrate smoothly. Now that she had Dex, she was not willing to let him go just because his brother was being an ass. She contemplated calling Claudia to talk it over with her, but remembered they were going out to dinner tonight with her parents to tell them about the baby and the quicker wedding date. At least they'd be having fun.

She could have called May, or even Jocelyn, but she really just wanted to be quiet and breathe in the silence. Life was going to be messy for a little while after this, she knew it and accepted it. Ethan was completely set against her, and part of her understood it. He'd grown up with a man who thought he had to do it all himself. That was bound to have rubbed off on him to some extent. She would simply have to work hard to meld with them. She wasn't afraid of that hard work, especially if it meant a lifetime with Dex, watching Phoebe grow into a beautiful young lady.

Around midnight, she realized that maybe their conversation was more intense than Dex had anticipated. They'd had a lot to talk about, and she didn't expect him to call a halt to it just to check in with her.

She turned off her lights and headed to a bed that

felt a lot bigger now. Bigger and lonely. Hopefully, not for much longer.

She kept her phone close, just in case, though. She didn't care if he called at two in the morning, she'd answer.

****

It was twelve-thirty, and Dex's eyes were bleary. He and Ethan had gone round and round about Zoe and the baby and his responsibility. Nothing was solved, but at least they were talking, and Ethan was home.

"Please don't leave again without letting me know," he said as they parted ways at the top of the stairs.

"I won't." Ethan kicked at the carpet. "Can you put her in her crib and keep the monitor for tonight? I've been sleeping in my car for two weeks. I want to stretch out. I'll take tomorrow night."

"Fine." It was a step in the right direction. One Dex was not going to shrug off. "Sleep well."

"I hope to." Ethan headed down the hallway, his steps slow and measured.

Dex put Phoebe into her crib, then kissed her goodnight after he tucked her in with her turtle and blanket. Ethan was going to love her once he got a chance to be with her. They'd make this work. They had to.

Morning came early enough, but not as early as Dex had expected. He rolled over in his too-big bed with the scent of Zoe in his nostrils and his thoughts fuzzy. The clock read a few minutes after nine. No way had Phoebe slept that long.

Jumping out of bed, Dex feared the worst, that Ethan had left with her in the middle of the night. That worry tripled when he didn't find her in her bed. Ethan's room was next. He whipped open the door to find Ethan sound asleep, curled around the little cooing girl. She raised her hands when she saw Dex and giggled.

Scooping her and her turtle into his arms, he kissed her cheeks and then her belly. "Let's let Daddy sleep, Phoebster."

He carried her down the stairs and into the kitchen on silent feet. Setting her in her high chair, he started coffee and took out some donuts he'd bought a couple of days ago. It would have to do. Mixing her food with some cereal, he looked out the kitchen window to find a car in his driveway that shouldn't be there.

It had been dark the night Delly dropped Phoebe off, but not so dark that he wouldn't recognize her car. And if he was right, it was sitting in his driveway. Shit. Was she back for the baby?

Part of him wanted to bolt every door and secure every window and not answer the doorbell if it rang. Dropping his head and staring into the stack of dirty dishes, he knew he'd never really do that.

He might as well get this over with now.

Taking Phoebe with him, he stalked out to the car and knocked on the window. "Delly?"

Her eyes were swollen, her nose red, and her hair a mess. He opened the door for her to come out.

"I'm sorry," she cried and fell into him, hugging both him and Phoebe at the same time. The little girl patted her head and she cried harder.

"Why don't you come in?"

"Are you sure?"

Why did everyone keep asking him that? "Yes, I'm

sure, or I wouldn't have offered. I only have coffee and donuts for breakfast, sorry."

"It's more than I've eaten since I talked to you the other day."

Well, that wasn't good. Surely he had some eggs or something he could whip up, too.

They entered the kitchen with Delly trailing along behind him. He'd started to put Phoebe back in her high chair when he felt Delly's soft hand lightly touch his arm. "May I?"

A part of him hesitated, but the other part knew what he had to do. "Sure."

He made small talk while he scrambled eggs and pulled some bacon from the freezer. He wanted to give her a couple of minutes to settle in before he started the interrogation. And watching her with her daughter was a revelation. The way she touched her face over and over again, kissed the top of her head, sniffed her hair, all with tears silently streaming down her face.

This was not the young woman who had slammed out of his house three weeks ago. Did she regret the decision she'd made in anger and haste? Would she want Phoebe back? He knew he wasn't going to let her take the baby again. He had legal documentation that she had given her up. He'd wave that around if he had to. He was not going to make Phoebe live as he had, being bounced back and forth when your parents thought it was convenient to take you out of the place you wanted to call home.

Ethan chose that moment to emerge from upstairs. Dex's plan had been to get some food in front of Delly and then go talk to Ethan, but that, as most of his other plans lately, went awry.

"What are you doing here?" Ethan snatched Phoebe out of her mother's arms and scared her.

"Give her back. Look what you did!"

Phoebe was bawling in earnest now. Dex stepped in and took her from Ethan. "The two of you knock it off and be quiet until the eggs are done, and then we'll talk."

They both sat glaring at each other as Dex kept on with the eggs, showing Phoebe how to crack an egg one-handed and making her laugh when he used the whisk. The strangest things intrigued her.

The pan was hot enough to sizzle when he poured the beaten eggs in. Within minutes he had Phoebe back in her high chair and eggs and bacon in front of everyone.

"First we're going to eat, and then we're going to talk. Like the adults we are. A conversation, not a shouting match, not a pissing contest, but a real conversation. Stuff your mouth until you're ready to do that. I don't want screaming in front of Phoebe. It upsets her, and we've done that enough lately, don't you think?"

Two identical nods, and then Phoebe joined in while she banged her spoon on the high chair table.

They ate in silence. Dex kept his eyes on his plate. If Ethan and Delly were shooting daggers at each other with their eyes, he did not want to see it.

He took his plate to the sink when he was done, and they both followed suit. They all sat down with cups of coffee, and looks were exchanged around the table. Even Phoebe looked from one to the next.

"I'll start, then." Dex cradled his cup in his hands. "Thank you for telling Ethan to come home, Delly. I appreciate it. The issue we were facing, mainly your mother trying to take Phoebe away, has been handled. Zoe and I went to her lawyer's office to discuss it with her. She will no longer be seeking custody."

"That woman went with you?" Ethan sneered.

"Yes, 'that woman' did, and I'm glad she did."

"Is she the one who put Cathy in her place?" Delly asked. When Dex nodded, she turned to Ethan. "Cathy about had a cow. She was screaming about some bitch bilking her out of the money she should have gotten for letting me live there before she kicked me out the last time."

Ethan merely grunted, and Delly turned back to Dex. "I'd like to thank her, if I can. I don't think anyone has ever put Cathy in her place so effectively. She was seething."

"Zoe did an amazing job."

"Zoe, Zoe, Zoe. I'm sure she's a pure angel," Ethan said. "But that's not what we're talking about." He glared at Dex, then Delly. "Why the hell are you here? You walked out without more than ten words and signed the kid over to me, and yet here you are, eating our food and looking at the kid like you missed her."

Dex kicked Ethan under the table.

"And here you are after taking off for almost three weeks to what? Find yourself? Decide if you were man enough to take on a child you helped make?"

"Children, children." Dex wanted to lay his head down on the table. He gripped the edge of the wood, instead. "This is the part where we become adults." He eyed both of them. "Delly, sweetheart, why are you here? You look like you slept out in your car in the driveway last night. What time did you get here?"

She fiddled with a napkin and refused to meet his eyes. "About 12:15. I was going to knock, because all the lights were on, but then they started going off one by one, so I thought I'd wait until morning."

"And to the first question? Why are you here?"

Ethan opened his mouth and Dex said, "Shut it. It'll be your turn soon enough."

Delly shredded the napkin. "I can't do this. I can't leave her with you guys. I'm sure she'd have a much better life with the two of you, it's why I brought her in the first place, but I just can't be without her. The last three weeks have about killed me." She started crying. "When Cathy kicked me out, we moved from one friend's house to another for almost a month before I realized that I couldn't keep doing that to Phoebe. I wanted better for her. So I got mad at myself, at the world, and brought her here. I signed over my rights because I didn't want to be able to come back. But I didn't realize how hard it was going to be, and now I need her back."

"Do you have a place to stay? A job? How are you going to care for her?" Dex said this gently, but he needed to know her answers.

"I don't know. I'll figure something out."

"You can't drop her off and then pick her up over and over again, Delly." Ethan exploded from his chair, pacing like a caged tiger. "I might have run out, but I'm back to stay now, and she's mine. You gave her to me and Dex, and I will raise her. We don't need you. We don't need anyone."

"Ethan, please, sit. Phoebe's getting agitated."

They all looked at the glassy eyes of the little girl sitting in her high chair with a stranglehold on her turtle.

"Sorry." He flopped back in his chair. "But I'm not lying. We'll raise her, Dex, and it'll be good. You did a good job with me. You and I can do a better job together with her."

"Ethan..."

"What? We can make this work. We made it. We'll make it again." He drummed his fingers on the table.

"We did make it, but I think I forgot something. The ability to trust and to realize you don't always have to go it on your own. I'd still be fighting Cathy if it hadn't been for Zoe. And though I know you don't want to hear her name again, she's the one who's been taking care of Phoebe every day while I work. Every day, Ethan. What are we going to do without help? Phoebe's not twelve, like you were. She can't take care of herself at all."

"Fine, Zoe can stay the nanny, but Delly doesn't get to walk in and out. And you and Zoe stay away from each other. I'll drop her off and pick her up."

"Why are you being like this, Ethan?" Delly jumped in. "You weren't like this when we were together."

"Were we really together, Delly? You sure did let me walk away easily enough. You didn't even flinch when I told you I was moving." He stabbed his finger at the table with a thump.

"If you'd count back, that's about the time I found out I was pregnant, you idiot. You leaving just made it easier to not have to tell you I'd forgotten to take my pills for a few days. I thought I'd just raise her myself. At least then I'd have someone who would always love me and never leave me."

Wow. Dex felt that hit in the solar plexus for Ethan, who looked green.

She continued. "I never had anyone love me until you, Ethan, and even that was over soon enough. When I found out I was pregnant with Phoebe, I built all kinds of dreams in my head. She and I would be a team like you and Dex. We'd live together, and she'd look to me for everything. I'd provide the kind of life and love that I never got. I knew I'd be good at it. And then Cathy started getting mean again. Another mouth in the house. She wouldn't touch the baby, or help me at all. And then she kicked me out when I wouldn't go after your brother for child support. Hell, she wanted me to say that the baby wasn't even yours but Dex's. That he'd raped me and I wanted money, so she wouldn't ever have to work again. And then I could keep the brat." She was crying in earnest now, tears streaming down her face and sobs choking her. "I brought her to you to get her away from that, knowing you and Dex would love her. And then you fucking left and jaunted off like it was no big deal. Well, it was a big deal. It still is. And I'll figure something out this time. Maybe I can get a job around here and rent a room. But I'm not leaving again, so deal with it."

Phoebe was drooping in her high chair, so Dex scooped her out of the chair and turned to the two teenagers who were being forced to be adults. "I'm going to take Phoebe up to her crib. Why don't you tell her where I found the baby this morning, Ethan? I'll be right down."

He took a breather upstairs and rested his forehead against the crib railing as he heard the murmur of voices from below. At least it wasn't shouting. This would all work out somehow. He'd caught Ethan more than once saying Delly's name in his sleep, and he knew he still cared for the girl who'd wrung his heart for over a year. Maybe this was the break they needed to make things work. And if she ended up living in his house? Honestly, he wouldn't mind. There was enough room, and that meant Phoebe would still be under his roof and eating his three squares.

Chapter Eighteen

By Monday afternoon, Zoe had stopped toting her phone around with her. It had been three days since Dex was supposed to call her. Perhaps he and Ethan were still working out details, but he should have at least had two minutes to text her. Instead she had nothing and was tired of waiting around.

He hadn't sent a bouquet, either. It was like he'd dropped off the face of the earth. While she understood he had a lot going on, she also knew that she shouldn't be that easily ignored, not if she truly meant anything to him.

This was worse than being the pickle jar loosener. At least then she knew it really wasn't her, it was them. She'd never invested herself in a relationship like this. This was more like hell, and it hurt. So much.

"Get back here!" Claudia called through the office door.

Zoe was totally not in the mood for an emergency girl meeting, so she ignored Claudia.

"I can bring it out there," she threatened in her mom voice.

"Fine." She waved to her mom to let her know she'd be right back and stomped into the office. "I want nothing to do with any meetings, or well-meaning advice. I get that he has a lot going on, but he could have at least texted or called." She heaved a breath.

"Does that cover it all?"

"Have you tried to call him?" Claudia crossed her ankles on the edge of the desk.

"No. He said he'd call me, and he would have if he was going to. I'm not chasing anyone, Claudia."

"This is different, Zoe. I know that thing with the married man several years ago upset you and when you went after him you found out about the wife and kids, but that's not the surprise at the end of this tunnel."

Zoe gasped. She'd never told anyone the truth about Kevin.

"You don't have secrets from me, girly. That's how I know you're in love with Dex, and that you're crying at night. Please, go get him."

"No, he'll have to come get me. On his knees."

"And will you take him if he does?"

"That remains to be seen."

****

Dex waved at Zoe through the front window of Decadence an hour after they'd closed on Monday. He'd been trying to get hold of her for the last hour and a half, but she wasn't answering his calls. And when he'd called the shop, May kept telling him she wasn't there. So he'd decided to come down and see for himself when he was finished with work for the day.

He was in a shit ton of trouble anyway, as well he should be. He'd let three days go by without giving her a call. With Delly moving in and Ethan and Delly patching things up, and learning to parent together, he had an excuse, but it wasn't good enough, even in his own mind.

Many times since he'd seen her to the door with that kiss he'd second-guessed himself about not letting

186

her stay. He'd chosen Ethan because he'd had to, but he should have forced Ethan to deal with his life with her by his side. He'd thought he'd walk in, apologize, and all would be right. Well, that was his hope, anyway.

Until he saw her standing behind her counter with her arms crossed and a mulish expression on her lovely face.

He knocked on the glass and pantomimed her opening the door. She shook her head and sneered at him. Damn, if he didn't find even that expression intriguing. He had it bad.

But she stood on the inside, not budging an inch. He tugged his cell phone from his belt, then pressed the speed dial number for Decadence. He could hear the phone ringing inside from his position on the sidewalk, but she just shook her head again, not answering.

His frustration level was peaking even as he tried to control it. He didn't know what kind of game she was playing, but it was fast becoming annoying. He might have been a jerk for not calling for over three days, but he had a legitimate reason, dammit.

Looking up, he saw the lights on upstairs and prayed his hunch would prove right when he dialed the apartment on the second floor. His call was answered on the first ring.

"Hello?"

"Claudia?"

"Dex, is that you standing down on the sidewalk?" She laughed a throaty laugh. The sound was interesting, but did nothing for him, unlike the scowl that still marred Zoe's face. He was perverse.

He shook his head, never taking his eyes off his quarry. And it was a good sign, or at least he thought it was, that Zoe never took her eyes off him, either.

"Yes, it's me. I can see Zoe inside the store, but she won't come to let me in."

"Hmmmm. I was wondering what she was still doing down there when we were supposed to be having dinner."

"That's not helping." He paced back and forth in front of the door, swinging his gaze back and forth to keep Zoe in sight.

"I'm not sure why I should help you when you've obviously forgotten that you had my sister's heart in your hands."

He had? He was hoping they'd start dating and eventually she would belong to him, but if she already did, then he was in even deeper than he thought. "Shit!"

"You know, I don't have to listen to you swear, Mr. Zegray."

"No, no. I'm sorry." He rubbed a hand at his forehead and blew out a breath. "I apologize for swearing. Please don't hang up."

"I wasn't planning on it. But my curiosity is the only thing keeping me on the line. So explain yourself, and I might see what I can do about letting you in the back way."

"Give me ten minutes, and I'm going to come back. Delly, Phoebe's mom, came home, and so did Ethan. They're working things out and are both going to live with me and Phoebe. It's been hectic, but I never should have let it go on this long." Pacing was wearing him out, so he stopped and just rested a hand on the wood frame of a window.

"You might have wanted to at least text, you know."

"I know, I know, but I didn't, and now all I can do is apologize."

"It had better be a good one. Run down to the grocery store, since all the other florists are closed now. Get her something meaningful. Now," Claudia said.

****

Zoe felt safe from intrusion by Dex because Decadence was equipped with an internal system that let them know with an electronic buzz when someone came into the store through the back or front door. It could be heard in any room, even in the flower cooler, where Zoe stood trying to cool off her head. She would have dunked her head in a bucket of water if she'd thought it would do any good.

Because, despite the fact she was mad as all hell at Dex for ignoring her, she still couldn't deny the way her body had heated when he'd knocked on the window. Or the way her knees threatened to melt when his penetrating stare zoomed through the glass. She could even admit—inside her brain only, of course—that she still wanted him, even after he'd neglected to get in touch with her at all.

Oh, God, but the way he'd stood outside, leaning his forehead against the window frame, his eyes down and his cell phone to his ear. There was something so incredibly sexy about him that really snagged her right in the stomach.

Well, regardless, she was done with him. He'd even had the nerve to make another call after she wouldn't answer the store phone.

Then the door buzzed. She knew Dex had no way of getting into the store, so it must be Claudia. And did she have an earful for her sister.

She came out of the walk-in refrigerator laughing. But the sound abruptly stopped when she came face to face with Dex. He swept her into his arms before she could draw her next breath, and his lips were on hers in the same heartbeat.

His mouth played with hers. He licked at the seam of her lips until she knew he wanted her to open to him. A small fuzzy part of her brain willed her to give in to the urge to do just that. But the bigger part of her resisted.

She pressed her hands against his chest, fully intending to push him away. But her body had other plans. Her fingers ended up curling into his suit jacket and pulling him to her. She opened her mouth, even though she hadn't intended to give him the satisfaction.

And then she was lost. All thoughts of him being another pickle jar flew out of her head as her blood heated and her head swam with the deliciousness of the taste of mint on his tongue and the way his fingers trailed into the fine hairs at her neck. He kissed with his whole body, his hips rocking into hers, his leg insinuating its way between her thighs. On and on it went until she didn't know which way was up.

But when his hand went to her breast, she drew in a breath through her nose and pushed him away. "I can't do this. You need to leave." She turned away, bracing her hands on the counter and trying to breathe normally with her heart pounding to beat the band. "How did you get in anyway?"

Not that she wanted to stand around and have a conversation with him, but she knew she'd locked the doors.

"Your wonderful sister let me in."

She didn't turn to look at him as the boil in her blood went from desire to burning rage. "She what?"

"She let me in because she listened to my sob story, gave me some advice, and then let me in when I made the right decision."

She didn't want to face him because she didn't know what she'd do—melt or yell. She expected she'd yell.

She did not, however, expect to be presented with a big bouquet of flowers. From behind her, his arm snaked around and handed her a bouquet. The clutch of amaranth, lemon blossoms, magnolia, pink carnations, bridal roses, and red tulips was big enough that she'd have to borrow an urn from down here to put them in her house. The bunch of flowers itself was not exactly pretty, but she knew the meaning behind each bloom. She didn't know if the bearer did, though.

"You're going to have to take down the flowers if you want me to talk to you."

"I was hoping for a little leeway," Dex's beautiful voice said. It warmed her heart and made her toes curl.

But he wasn't supposed to be here, and he wasn't still supposed to be trying. He certainly wasn't supposed to be bringing her flowers that meant faithful love, endless love, respect, and affection. If he even knew what they meant.

And where the hell did he get them? She certainly hadn't filled an order like that in the last twenty-four hours.

She whipped around and stabbed him in the side with her finger. "Where did you get those?"

"Down at the grocery store."

She plopped her hands on her hips, not letting him

off the hook just yet. "You went to the *grocery store* and bought a bouquet?"

"Another bad move in a long list of bad moves," he said, bringing the flowers down and letting them hang inverted at his side. "I'll go." He turned and put action to his words. He looked so defeated she couldn't let him walk out.

"I didn't say I wouldn't take them."

He didn't turn around. He stood halfway to the front door and heaved a sigh. "I'm sorry for not calling."

Her heart broke a little. She'd made him sigh as if the world were coming to an end. "Do you even know what you have in your hands?"

He did turn around this time and pointed out each flower, not looking into her eyes. "Unfading love and immortality is the amaranth, fidelity in love from the lemon blossoms, magnolias are perseverance, woman's love are the pink carnation, happy love from the bridal roses, and my declaration of love is the red tulips."

Jeez, he really did know. And it touched something very deep inside her. Something she hadn't let out since she was fifteen years old and seeing her sister struggle to make things work while her life was turned around. But if Claudia had the courage to do that, and to keep picking up the pieces to have her perfect life, then Zoe could do it, too. No one said love wouldn't come looking, and she'd be a fool to turn a blind eye to a guy who'd carry around a bouquet of flowers like this and endure the grocery store to get them.

"Get in here so I can ravish you," she said, pulling him in by the ears. "And I think you really need to start thinking about what kind of ring you're going to put on my finger when we get married."

He laughed. "Yes, ma'am." He kissed her for a few minutes, then gently set her back. "There are a few more things to be discussed, though."

She locked her elbows against her side. Maybe she had been stupid to mention getting married.

"First off, I love you and would be happy to have you as my wife. No more pickle jar loosening for you."

She smiled. "Okay."

"Second, and this is a big one. The reason I haven't called is that Delly came back. She and Ethan are working things out. They burned the papers she wrote out giving up her legal rights. There's a long story there that I'll tell you, but you have to know going in that you're taking on a whole houseful."

"Anything, as long as you're part of the deal. I love you, too, Dex, in a way I never thought I would love anyone."

"Can I ask two questions, then?" He rested his forehead against hers.

"Yes and yes."

"Let me ask first."

She laughed. "Oh, sorry."

From his coat pocket he pulled a small jar of kosher pickles and handed it to her. "The first I'm taking regardless, but I'll ask anyway. Will you open my pickle jar?"

She would not cry. She would not cry. "I will gladly open your jar." And she popped the lid. Pickles weren't exactly the smell she would always want to associate with the day her life was complete, but she'd take it.

"You already said yes, so I wasn't taking no at this

point. The second, though, you might need to think about."

"Okay?"

"Can we keep your apartment above here so that we have a haven when the house gets to be too much?"

"Of course." Ever the practical man, that Dex Zegray of hers. And as long as he swept her off her feet practically every day, she was the luckiest woman on earth.

A word about the author...

Misty Simon loves a good story and decided one day that she would try her hand at it. Eventually she got it right. There's nothing better in the world than making someone laugh, and she hopes everyone at least snickers in the right places when reading her books.

She lives with her husband, daughter, and three insane dogs in Central Pennsylvania, where she is hard at work on her next novel or three.

She loves to hear from readers, so drop her a line at
misty@mistysimon.com
and visit at
www.mistysimon.com.